One Ye...

Four sisters, four seasons, four weddings!

When their father dies unexpectedly, the Waverly sisters are set to inherit the beloved outback family estate. The only problem? An arcane stipulation in the will that requires all four of them to be married within a year or they'll lose the farm for good! But with such little time, how on earth will they each find a husband? Well...

Matilda is secretly already married—to a *prince* no less! Now she just needs to track him down...
in *Secretly Married to a Prince*
by Ally Blake

Eve spends a night of distraction with a tattooed stranger, and the consequences are binding!
in *Reluctant Bride's Baby Bombshell*
by Rachael Stewart

Ana turns to her best friend for help.
But their marriage of convenience is quickly complicated by *in*convenient feelings...
in *Cinderella and the Tycoon Next Door*
by Kandy Shepherd

And Rose makes a deal with the devil:
the strip of land his family—and the Waverlys' longtime rivals—has been after for years in exchange for a temporary marriage!
in *Claiming His Billion-Dollar Bride*
by Michelle Douglas

All available now!

Dear Reader,

I had a cunning plan when I trotted off to the Romance Writers of Australia conference back in 2022—to convince Ally Blake and Kandy Shepherd to write a series together. So when I saw Ally sitting alone enjoying a quiet glass of bubbles, I casually sat down with a "Hey, I've been thinking..."

Luckily she loved the idea as much as I did, and we soon had Kandy and Rachael on board. We fell in love with our premise. *Four sisters who need to marry within a year to save the family cattle station? Yes, please!* And then a strange thing happened—a chemistry developed between the four of us, a certain synergy, and it lent the project the most wonderful energy. We moved each other to tears more than once when we shared key scenes, made each other laugh and happy sigh.

A big chunk of my heart will now always belong to Matilda, Eve, Ana and Rose—our marvelous, bighearted sisters. I hope these stories touch your hearts and move you as much as they have Ally, Rachael, Kandy and me.

Hugs,
Michelle

CLAIMING HIS BILLION-DOLLAR BRIDE

MICHELLE DOUGLAS

ROMANCE

Harlequin®
ROMANCE

ISBN-13: 978-1-335-59671-0

Claiming His Billion-Dollar Bride

Copyright © 2024 by Michelle Douglas

Harlequin Enterprises ULC
22 Adelaide St. West, 41st Floor
Toronto, Ontario M5H 4E3, Canada
www.Harlequin.com

Printed in U.S.A.

Michelle Douglas has been writing for Harlequin since 2007 and believes she has the best job in the world. She lives in a leafy suburb of Newcastle, on Australia's east coast, with her own romantic hero, a house full of dust and books, and an eclectic collection of '60s and '70s vinyl. She loves to hear from readers and can be contacted via her website, michelle-douglas.com.

Books by Michelle Douglas

Harlequin Romance

One Summer in Italy

Unbuttoning the Tuscan Tycoon
Cinderella's Secret Fling

Singapore Fling with the Millionaire
Secret Billionaire on Her Doorstep
Billionaire's Road Trip to Forever
Cinderella and the Brooding Billionaire
Escape with Her Greek Tycoon
Wedding Date in Malaysia
Reclusive Millionaire's Mistletoe Miracle
Waking Up Married to the Billionaire

Visit the Author Profile page
at Harlequin.com for more titles.

To Ally, Rachael and Kandy. Ladies, you're absolute goddesses! I'm missing the daily emails, the flurry of questions, the brainstorming and the laughter. I heart you guys so hard. Wanna do it again sometime? :)

Praise for
Michelle Douglas

PROLOGUE

Garrison Downs,
June

ROSE STARED AT George Harrington who sat behind her father's desk in her father's chair and it took all of her strength not to stand up and yell at him to get out from behind it. The aging family lawyer didn't deserve that. He'd checked with her first, had asked her permission. It made sense that he sat where the rest of the room could see him.

But it still felt like sacrilege.

Glancing out of the French windows at the ancient gums, golden grasses and red dirt in the middle distance, she searched for calm, aching to turn and clasp Tilly's hand, but afraid if she did she might actually burst into ugly sobs. She wouldn't freak Tilly out like that. Concentrating on her breathing, she sent Tilly all the *buck-up, you're-not-alone* sister vibes that she could.

For the past month, she and her sisters had survived the shock of their father's death, the national outpouring of grief that had followed, and all the pomp and ceremony of a state funeral. Only allowing themselves to grieve in tiny pockets of downtime. For Holt Waverly, their father, had been a national icon, a legend, and everyone had wanted to claim him as their own.

Everyone had had a story they'd wanted to tell. Everyone had wanted their share of the… In her darker moments she called it drama, but she knew it was a combination of shock and grief—lesser than hers admittedly, but real nonetheless. She'd managed to say all that was right and appropriate when cameras had flashed in her face half blinding her, microphones shoved under her nose and questions barked at her.

'Your father's death must've come as a shock?'

'How much of an impact will this have on Garrison Downs?'

'You must be missing him?'

She'd had to steel herself over and over. Calling the media morons wouldn't help anyone, it wouldn't do Holt proud. And she'd do him proud now if it killed her.

As aware as she was of Tilly on the sofa behind her, she was equally aware of Eve on the big screen on the back wall, video-conferencing in from her office in London.

A bitter smile twisted through her. When she said she and her sisters had got through the shock and ordeal of the last month, she meant she and

Tilly. Eve hadn't been here. Eve hadn't come home. Not even for the funeral.

Rose had reconciled herself to never knowing what had happened between Eve and their father, but to not come home…to not—

Don't think about that now.

Once this will-reading was done, she could stride out of here and make sure the section of fence at Devil's Bend had been fixed, get an update on Jasper's swollen fetlock, ensure that Aaron, her head stockman, had a handle on the bore-running rota she'd set up, and that Ricky and Blue, the new station hands, were keeping their late-night partying within limits. The boys were young, but complaints had been made and there were phone calls from fretting mothers to negotiate. After that she really needed to make a start on the backlog of correspondence, schedule an appointment with the accountant, and at some point next week she needed to check in with Franz Arteta about their contract.

There was *so* much to do. Her father had made it look easy, but it wasn't. At least, it wasn't for her. How on earth was she supposed to fill such big shoes? How—?

Don't think about that now.

She refocussed on the view outside again. There were too many people in the room—she could see their reflections in the window glass as they moved—and George Harrington's voice droned on and on.

Bequests were made to various agricultural organisations, and the academic and industry-based research projects Holt had sponsored, a generous donation made to the arts—no doubt in honour of Tilly, which briefly made her smile—and an ongoing commitment pledged to the fund set up in their mother's name for cancer research.

Eventually George paused, cleared his throat. 'To my daughters, I leave all my worldly possessions not listed hereupon, including, but not limited to, the entirety of Garrison Downs.'

The voice seemed to come from a long way away. And now that the reading of the will was drawing to a close, Rose contrarily wanted to slow time. These were the last words her father would ever speak to her. She wasn't ready. He should still be here laughing with them, offering advice in his quiet laconic way, riding out on his black stallion, Jasper, and living to a ripe old age here on the land he loved.

'Let it be known that it is my wish that my eldest daughter, Rose Lavigne Waverly, take over full control of management of Garrison Downs. If that is *her* wish. If not, I bow to her choice.'

She flinched. She'd always expected to take over one day. Her father and grandfather had instilled in her a deep love of the land, had groomed her to one day take up the reins of Garrison Downs.

But not yet.

'At this point, could we please clear the room,' George said, 'of everyone bar family?'

She let out a careful breath, didn't turn to watch as people filed out. Perhaps Dad had left them some final word—a loving message meant for their ears only.

George took off his glasses and rubbed his hand across his forehead.

She leaned forward.

'There is a condition placed over the bequest. One that has been attached to the property since its transfer to your family years ago.'

George laid his glasses on top of the papers in front of him. 'As I'm sure you know, the history of Garrison Downs is…complicated, what with your great-great-grandmother having won the land from the Garrison family in a poker game in 1904.'

That poker match had become local legend— one of those tales of derring-do that was bandied about whenever the beer flowed too freely. But it had also been the cause of a lot of ill will between the Waverly and Garrison families.

'Any time the land has been passed down since, certain conditions had to be met.' He read from the will directly. 'Any male Waverly heir, currently living, naturally inherits the estate.'

'Naturally,' Rose murmured, rolling her eyes.

'But,' George continued, 'if the situation arises

where there is no direct male heir, any and all daughters, of marrying age, must be wed within a year of the reading of the will, in order to inherit as a whole.'

She stared, tried to make sense of the words he'd uttered.

On the screen behind her, Eve laughed.

She swung around. 'You think this is *funny*?'

'I think it's hilarious, Rose. I mean, come on, what century do you think we're in, Harrington?'

Eve sounded so sure. Rose shook her head. This had to be someone's idea of a sick joke. 'What am I missing?'

'The land,' Tilly said quietly, 'is entailed to sons. If there is no son, the Waverly women can inherit, but only if all of us are married.'

Rose gripped the arms of her chair so hard her fingers started to ache. Then she leapt up to pace. 'That can't possibly be legal, not in this day and age. Surely?'

'Too right, it can't be,' Eve said, sounding battle-ready.

'It is…arcane,' said George. 'But it has been a part of the lore of this land for several generations. So far as I see it, and so far as your father must have wanted, it stands.'

She slammed her hands to her hips. 'How has this never come up before?'

'Sons,' said Tilly. 'Dad was an only child. Pop only had brothers, though one died of measles and the other drowned, meaning the farm passed straight to him. Waverlys have always been most excellent at having at least one strapping farm-loving son. Until us.'

Rose swung to Tilly, lifted her hands as if to say, *What the actual...?*

Tilly nodded, silently saying, *I know, right?*

But there was no time for that. She planted her feet, turned back. 'And what happens if we re-fuse to...marry?'

'If the condition is not met, the land goes back to the current head of the Garrison family. Clay Garrison.'

'That double-dealing, underhand, two-faced old goat can't tell the back end of a bull from the front.'

George winced. 'The son seems a reasonable sort—'

'*Lincoln?* If he stopped partying long enough to even notice the level of responsibility coming his way...' She pressed her palms to her eyes and tried to stop treacherous toes from curling as pictures of Lincoln flooded her mind. 'If our land, our home, the business that we've built—' *that her father had built* '—fell into their hands, I—I can't even think it.'

This land was her destiny and had been ever since she'd understood what that word meant. She couldn't let her father down, Pop, all the Waverlys before her...or the generations of Waverlys to come. A wave of dizziness shook her and she braced her hands on her knees, forced herself to breathe slowly and deeply.

'Don't waste your time worrying about it, Rose, because it isn't going to happen,' Eve assured her from the screen. 'Not now. Not ever.'

George's gaze moved from her to Tilly…and Eve…and to the far wall. 'As it stands, unless all four of Holt Waverly's daughters are married within twelve months of the reading of this document—'

'Twelve months?' Rose straightened. 'But I can't… I'm not… I mean, none of us are even *seeing* anyone right now. Are we? Eve? Tilly?'

Tilly shook her head.

Rose went to glance at the screen but stopped herself at the last moment. What was the point? Eve shared so little of herself these days.

'Wait.' Tilly sat bolt upright. 'Back up a second. You said *four* daughters. There are only three of us.'

Rose followed Tilly's gaze to a slight dark-haired woman she hadn't noticed, sitting in their mother's chair. The young woman rose.

'Who are you?' Tilly asked, not unkindly. But then Tilly was constitutionally incapable of unkindness. It was one of the things they all loved about her.

The unknown woman swallowed, looking as if she wished herself a million miles away. 'Ana.'

'Who are you talking to, Tilly?' Eve said. 'I can't see.'

Her father's chair squeaked as George raced out from behind the desk, moving towards this Ana, his hand outstretched. 'Come forward, girl.'

Ana moved forward with a hesitant step.

'Anastasia, this is Matilda Waverly.' George smiled at Tilly. 'That there is Rose. And up on the screen is Evelyn. Girls, this is Anastasia Horvath.'

All the hairs on Rose's arms lifted. *Four* daughters.

No, that couldn't—

'Ana, here, is your father's daughter. Your half-sister. And therefore, according to your father's will…'

The rest of George's words faded away. *Half-sister!*

Spots formed in front of her eyes. The room spun. She'd known her parents' marriage had experienced rocky moments, but her father had adored his wife. He'd adored *them*. He'd have never…

But Anastasia's eyes were the same piercing blue as hers, Tilly's and Eve's. As Holt's. And George would know. He'd *know* the truth. He'd never allow an imposter to claim part of Holt Waverly's legacy.

George collapsed to the arm of the velvet sofa saying something about them still having their trusts and being wealthy women in their own rights. 'But the land itself, the Garrison Downs station and all of its holdings, will belong to the Garrison family unless you, Rose, Evelyn, Matilda, *and* Anastasia, are all married within the next twelve months.'

Even Ana was expected to shoulder this ridiculous burden?

When she'd never been allowed to be a part of their lives?

Reaching out, Rose grabbed the back of her chair, pieces of a giant jigsaw puzzle assembling themselves in her mind, falling into place—making a picture she didn't want to see.

'Rose?' Tilly started.

'Hang on, Evie.' She lifted her head to meet Eve's eyes fully for the first time in too long. 'Did you *know*? Is this why—?'

'I have to go,' said Eve just before her face abruptly disappeared as she disconnected from the call. Rose stared at the blank screen, her chest burning. Evie had known about her father's affair.

Oh, Evie, you shouldn't have had to bear that on your own.

She clenched her hands so hard she started to shake. How dared he? How dared her father keep a sister from them?

She stared at the door, willing him to walk through it and explain, to make things right somehow. A harsh laugh scraped her throat raw. An impossibility. An impossibility even if he were still alive!

Clenching her hands, she started for the door. If she didn't get out of here, she'd explode, and nobody in the room deserved that. 'I can't—I don't have time for this. I have a station to run.'

But before she strode out of the door she pointed at Ana. 'Stay!' She barked it like an order, as she would at some cocky station hand who'd tested her authority. She didn't mean to sound so bossy, but her voice was beyond control.

Continuing through the door, she hollered, 'Lindy, can you see that the yellow suite is made up for Anastasia, please? She'll be staying with us for a bit.'

CHAPTER ONE

ROSE STRODE INTO Holt's office, seized the calendar from the wall and counted the days down to the big red X marked in June.

Ninety days.

Ninety days! What the freaking heck...?

Flipping back, she counted again. Why had she left it so long?

Tilly had married her Henri and was a *princess*—oozing ecstasy and joy as was her wont. Evie was blissfully married to Nate with a baby on the way. And now Anastasia, who she'd not have blamed for clutching her trust fund to her chest and running for the hills—

She spun to glare at Holt's chair, but she didn't rant and rail at him as she had the day of his will-reading. She didn't speak to him at all. 'Beat the crap out of him, Pop,' she murmured instead.

She didn't know if other people spoke to their dead, but she'd spoken to her grandfather ever since he'd died when she was nineteen. Her grandmother, not so much. Unless it was to point out the stupidity of all of Katherine's previous strident advice. Her mother she'd chat to in the garden—telling her how her roses were coming along, describing the scent of the jasmine as the heat of a spring day cooled...telling her how much she missed her.

Swinging away, she slapped the calendar against her leg before hanging it back on the wall. Ana hadn't turned her back on them. Instead she was now married to her childhood friend, Connor, and so in love it hurt.

Her sisters had *all* met the terms of that stupid conditional bequest. Which meant Rose was now last man—*woman*—standing. If she didn't want to let her sisters down, she had to marry. If she didn't want to lose her home, she had to marry.

And the thought of losing Garrison Downs...

Reaching up, she retied her ponytail with fingers that shook. She *couldn't* let that happen.

Glaring at the calendar, she tilted her chin. 'Ninety days.' Not impossible. She pushed her shoulders back and swallowed. 'Piece of cake.'

'Talking to yourself again, Rose?'

Eve sauntered into the office in all her maternal contentment and smug in-loveness, and it made Rose want to laugh and wrap her sister in a bear-hug. 'I don't get as much sense from anyone else.' She nodded at Evie's glorious baby bump. 'But when you pop out my niece I might finally get some decent conversation around here.'

Eve grinned, but sobered when she glanced at the calendar. 'You don't have to marry. You know that, right?'

Just like Evie to cut straight to the chase. But…

Of course she had to marry. It was the only honourable thing to do. With Evie finally making Garrison Downs her home again, after it had taken so long to lure her back… Oh, no, Rose wasn't risking that.

Reaching out, she traced a finger across that big red X. 'But I believe I'm going to.' She'd do whatever necessary to keep Garrison Downs.

'You haven't been on a single date in the last nine months. You spend all your time with cattle and stockmen—' Evie broke off, eyes narrowing. 'You can't marry Aaron.'

She turned, curious to hear her sister's objections to her marrying Garrison Downs' head stockman. 'Why not?'

'He's fifteen years older than you!'

'So?'

'And he's being a pig to you at the moment.'

'I have it in hand.' Though, in truth, it was taking longer and proving trickier than expected. Holt would've had it sorted already—

She cut the thought dead, but not before a bone-crushing weight slammed down on her shoulders.

'And I saw him and Lindy looking very cosy the other night.'

Ah, a romance was brewing between Aaron and their housekeeper…

'Aaron was Plan B.' And he could just as easily be replaced with Johnno or Nick or one of the other stockmen.

'Then who on earth is Plan A?'

Folding her arms, she leaned back against the desk, the plan that had been brewing in her mind for the last few months emerging in a starburst of decision. 'Lincoln Garrison.' Energy powered through her when she said his name, lifting the weight from her shoulders and tossing it to the four winds.

'Linc Garrison?' Evie's jaw dropped. 'Are you mad?'

'Okay, Rose, you're going to be cool, calm and collected.' Dragging in a breath, Rose did all that she could to turn herself into the epitome of unflappable self-possession.

Don't forget sassy.

The façade slipped. What the hell…? *'No!'* The word echoed in the chopper's tiny cabin. *Jeez*, this was real life, not a soap opera.

Go on, Lincoln would like sassy. Channel your favourite soap-opera heroines.

A reluctant smile tugged at her lips. What she was about to do would make a great plot line in any of her beloved soaps—*The Bold and the Beautiful, Coronation Street, Home and Away*—

but she needed to keep things sensible and businesslike.

And that was what this was—a business proposition. Marrying Lincoln would safeguard Garrison Downs' future. What was more, it would help her accomplish another objective. If she and Lincoln married, if they came to know one another better—and in an ideal world became friends—they could bring the ridiculous feud between their families to an end.

In the scrub below a mob of kangaroos were startled from their morning siesta and scattered, their red-grey coats gleaming in the sun. From her current position, she couldn't see a single dwelling, though one of their stock camps would soon come into view. The cattle stations in the South Australian outback were seriously isolated. Out here neighbours ought to pull together. It'd be in both Garrison Downs' and Kalku Hills' best interests, and the district's, if she and Lincoln could learn to work together.

And while she'd never say it out loud, not even under the threat of torture, she couldn't help wondering if the Waverlys owed the Garrisons some kind of reparation. The way Louisa May had acquired the station, the bad blood it had created…the rumours that Louisa May Waverly had cheated Cordelia Garrison of the land. None of it had sat well with her.

Forty minutes later she landed the chopper in

the home paddock of Kalku Hills, as Lincoln had directed her to in his email. She noted his blue Cessna parked on the airstrip to her left and an army of butterflies gathered beneath her breast-bone.

Don't be silly. She had nothing to be nervous about. She was simply presenting a business prop-osition. Nothing more. *Be cool. Be calm. Be busi-nesslike.*

As if her thoughts had conjured him, Lincoln appeared on the homestead's veranda, ready to welcome her. A giant of a man at six feet four, and all of it broad hard muscle. Folding his arms, he leaned against a veranda post and she let out a long, slow breath.

Lincoln's movements were always unhurried, almost lazy, as if he had all the time in the world. As if it was too much of an effort to exert himself. Even when playing cricket he preferred to hit a boundary over pushing himself to run.

Today he wore suit trousers and a business shirt, and she thanked whatever God had prompted Evie to insist that she wear a little black skirt and a pale blue blouse. And black court shoes that were immediately covered in red dust when she leapt down to the ground.

She might not be at home in the fancy rags, but she was at home in the red dust. And while the business proposition she'd come to discuss might not be conventional, it was practical…and sound. And it was time.

Giving herself no further time to rehearse what she'd say, or consider what Lincoln's reaction might be once she'd said it, Rose moved in the direction of the homestead and the man waiting there, his hair glinting gold in the sunlight.

The homestead at Kalku Hills was sandstone, and it was big and beautiful in its own way. But it wasn't built on the same scale as the Garrison Downs homestead. There were no gardens, no pool, no frills. Though, as Clay's wife—Lincoln's mother—had left him twenty years ago, Rose suspected creature comforts weren't a high priority for the Garrison men.

'It's nice to see you, Rose.'

Lincoln held out his hand when she reached him and she shook it, her mouth going dry. It was always like this, the immediate physical impact, whenever she drew too close to him, as if time were simultaneously speeding up and slowing down. 'Hello, Lincoln.'

He didn't let her go immediately. Dark eyes travelled lazily across her face and something inside her trembled. No doubt he clocked the dark circles beneath her eyes and the fact she wore no make-up. Lincoln had dated some of the nation's most beautiful women. Word on the street was that he was a man with a discerning eye and a short attention span.

What the hell was she doing here? For a moment she was tempted to wheel away and speed back to Garrison Downs. A woman like her could never tempt a man like him.

Going to play the craven little virgin now?

That had her pushing her shoulders back. She had plenty to tempt him—namely land. Lincoln Garrison might be a freewheeling playboy, but he wasn't an idiot. He'd recognise a good deal when he saw one. And while he might be as hot as sin this was a *business* meeting.

'It's *really* nice to see you, Rose.'

She rolled her eyes. The man was also incapable of not flirting. And while she mightn't be blonde and busty, whenever he saw her Lincoln never failed to give her one of those lingering glances of appreciation that he seemed to save just for her. As he was doing right now.

For a moment she was tempted to flirt back, let herself imagine his expression if she allowed her gaze to make an equally slow perusal of his body. Because one question had always plagued her. What had seemed like a lifetime ago, Lincoln had asked her on a date. She'd declined, but she'd always wondered…

What if she'd said yes?

Her gaze lowered to take in the big, broad lines of him, and the pulse in her throat pounded. Maybe…

With a start she pulled herself back into straight lines, cleared her throat. 'So you already said.'

Those tempting lips tugged into a wider smile and it was all she could do not to groan. This would be so much easier if he looked like...*an ordinary man*!

'It was worth saying twice.' With the smallest hitch of his head, he led her inside, glancing back over his shoulder. 'You look great.' His gaze drifted down to her legs. 'You dressed up.'

'So did you. Don't walk into the wall, Lincoln.'

He was in no danger of walking into the wall, but she needed him to stop looking at her like that or she might just dissolve into a puddle at his feet.

'This is a business meeting,' she added as he gestured for her to take a seat in the office. 'I wanted to look good.'

She waited, kind of fatalistically, for him to say something smooth like, *You always look good*.

'Why?'

She was glad when he didn't. 'Because I want you to say yes to the proposition I'm going to put to you.'

With a grin, he took the seat behind the desk. 'My reputation precedes me, huh? Show me a pair of pretty legs and I'm putty.'

He thought her legs were pretty?

Focus, Rose, focus.

When tea had been served, he lifted his mug to his mouth and surveyed her over the rim. 'I was intrigued when you requested a meeting. You said you had a proposal to put to me?'

'Yes, quite literally.'

Dark blond brows shot up. 'Literally?'

'As in precisely or exactly or accurately.' She sipped her tea before setting it on the desk. 'I've come to ask you to marry me, Lincoln.'

Lincoln Garrison was rarely lost for words. But he stared at Rose Waverly's composed and very beautiful face and couldn't think of a single thing to say.

He could think of plenty of things he'd like to do. Number one on that list was stride around the desk, pull her into his arms and kiss her until neither one of them could think straight. Nothing new in that, though. He had the same urge whenever he saw her.

One kiss. They'd shared one kiss. Seven years ago. It shouldn't have had such an impact.

But it had, and, determined to do something about the unfamiliar longings, the sleepless nights, the *need* that had burned through him, Lincoln had asked Rose out. He hadn't cared that she was a Waverly and he a Garrison. He hadn't thought she'd cared either.

He'd been wrong.

I'm sorry, Lincoln, I can't hurt my family like that. Please don't ask me again.

After that he'd given himself to a series of other

women, always hoping he'd find someone who'd fire his blood the way Rose did. He'd partied hard, had played up to the playboy image with which the tabloids had labelled him. It had amused him at the time. *Stupid.* Now most people wrote him off as shallow, bent only on pleasure.

Rose would too. Yet now she was asking him to *marry her*?

He clenched his hands to the underside of his desk, out of her sight, as he fought an unfamiliar dizziness. 'Did you just ask me to marry you?'

She nodded, as composed and in control as ever.

He refused to allow so much as a flickering eyelash to betray his disorientation. 'Why?' He eased back, stained his voice with amusement, but when she glanced down at her hands and went deathly still, he wished he hadn't. 'Why, Rose?' he repeated more gently.

Why would she ask him to marry her? Because, while he might've been hung up on her all these years, she sure as hell hadn't been hung up on him. He'd done his best not to take it personally. She hadn't appeared to be hung up on anyone.

Swallowing, she folded her hands in her lap and her pallor hit him. She'd lost weight since he'd last seen her—at Holt's funeral—nine months ago. Was she looking after herself? Did she have someone keeping an eye on her to make sure she wasn't working herself half to death?

He'd read the recent press release the family had issued, welcoming their half-sister Anastasia Horvath into the family. Holt's youngest daughter. To a woman not his wife. The news had rocked him. It had rocked the district. It had rocked *the nation*. Rose had been forced to deal with a lot these last few months. It hurt something inside him to see her looking so tired and drawn.

'Lincoln, I'm going to let you into a closely guarded secret.' He couldn't keep his brows from shooting up and she smiled weakly. 'I know relations between our two families haven't always been favourable.'

An understatement if there ever was one.

'But fences ought to be mended. And I figure we need to start somewhere.'

He leaned towards her. 'By you and me marrying?' Had he stepped into some alternate universe?

Just for a moment her gaze drifted to his shoulders and she moistened her lips as if suddenly parched.

Things inside him clenched.

Giving herself a shake, she dragged her gaze back to his. 'I ought to clarify that when I say marriage, I mean a mutually beneficial business arrangement. A temporary agreement. A paper marriage.'

He sat back, any desire to ease her nerves dissolving. 'Do go on,' he drawled.

To her credit, she kept her head high and her gaze steady. 'What I'm going to tell you now, Lincoln, is in the strictest of confidence.'

'Why would you trust me?'

She stared at him for a long moment. 'Sometimes you have to choose to believe the best in people. You and I *don't* have to carry on Holt and Clay's animosity. I'm very much hoping we won't.'

And there it was—her honesty…her decency—the reason he'd been unable to prevent his feelings from becoming tangled up in her in the first place. Why what he felt for her had always been more than physical. Rose was tough and capable and equipped in every way to run a huge operation like Garrison Downs, but what no one else seemed to see was how… It sounded biblical, which probably went to show how bad he had it for this woman, but how pure of heart Rose was.

'If you betray my trust… I guess that'll answer any question I have about the kind of man you are.'

'You can trust me, Rose. You have my word.'

Nodding, she moistened her lips again. 'There was a condition attached to my father's will, dating back to the time when Louisa May Waverly first acquired Garrison Downs.'

'When she won it in a poker game, you mean?'

'Yes.'

The poker game that had created so much ill will between the two families.

'The conditional bequest is old-fashioned. It states only a son can inherit the estate. If there are no sons then the daughters will inherit, but only if each daughter is married. They have twelve months from the reading of the will to fulfil the terms of the conditional bequest.'

The breath punched from his lungs. 'You *have to marry*?' She *had to marry* if she wanted to keep Garrison Downs? 'What kind of archaic…?' He tried to rein in his wild thoughts. 'Why are you asking *me*?'

For the briefest of moments her gaze fixed on his mouth and things inside him clenched and clashed. Her eyes darkened and he wondered if she was remembering that kiss they'd shared. It occurred to him now, with the space of the intervening years, that maybe it *had* rocked her world as much as it had his. Maybe it had shaken her so much it'd sent her running scared.

I can't hurt my family like that.

Both Rosamund and Holt were now dead. Rose's choices couldn't hurt them any more.

'Why am I asking you in particular?'

He crashed back to the here and now.

'Because if my sisters and I don't marry, the land will return to the current head of the Garrison family.'

He *couldn't* have heard her right.

'Which, obviously, is your father.'

Damn it all to hell!

He bit back something rude and succinct. His father couldn't get wind of this. If he did—

Rubbing a hand over his face, he banished the ugly images rising through him.

'Now, of course...' Rose's fingers formed a steeple '... I could marry one of the Downs' stockmen. Any one of them would do it to oblige me and I'll have fulfilled the conditional bequest.'

The thought of any one of them with Rose had his hands curling into fists.

'But...'

His heart pounded against the walls of his ribs. It took a superhuman effort to remain in his seat. 'But?'

Those extraordinary blue eyes met his, extraordinarily candid. 'It only seems fair to give you first right of refusal. I'd like to mend fences, Lincoln. I'd like us to be friends.'

'No, Rose, you want us to be husband and wife.'

'A *paper* marriage, though, Lincoln.' She seized her tea, took a huge gulp. 'We'd be friends who temporarily marry for mutual benefit, and then remain friends afterwards. I'd like the future generations of Waverlys and Garrisons to get along, wouldn't you?'

Yes.

Her nose wrinkled. 'I don't like your father.

Sorry. Hence the reason I'm asking *you* to marry me rather than him.'

He didn't like his father much sometimes either. And she couldn't marry Clay, couldn't give him even the smallest of opportunities to gain a foothold at Garrison Downs.

'And while I'm on the topic of people I don't like... My grandmother would've hated me to marry a Garrison. I know I should be above such things—' she gave a small grin, and he found an answering grin building inside him '—but apparently I'm not.'

'I didn't like your grandmother either.'

'She was a bitter woman.' She hesitated. 'Your father is becoming an awful lot like her.'

Her words burned a path through him, but only because they were true. Who else saw what Rose saw? If his father wasn't careful, he'd lose his standing in the district, and his reputation. Linc planned to do everything in his power to prevent that from happening.

In truth, Rose's proposal couldn't have come at a better time. If he wanted to prevent his father from making the biggest mistake of his miserable life, Rose had just handed him the means to do it. But he refused to appear too eager. Even he had his pride.

'Why should I say yes to this proposal of yours? I suspect as soon as the demands of the will are met and the estate passes to you and your sisters, you mean to divorce me.'

'As I said, this would be a business deal.' She clasped her hands lightly on the desk. 'You know that parcel of land my family has always refused to sell to Kalku Hills?'

Camels Bridge? That stretch of land linked two separate portions of Kalku Hills land. Owning it would allow easy movement between the two. It would save the station time, effort and money. What was more, that land came with water rights. It was, quite literally, worth its weight in gold. 'I know it well.'

'It would be your wedding present.'

He blew out a long breath. That was generous. *Really* generous. He couldn't resist the sport of seeing just how far he could push her, though. 'Would you consider throwing in your Angus bull?'

'Carnelian Boy?'

He nodded. The stud fees for him were phenomenal.

She hesitated. 'I wish I could say yes but I can't.'

Lifting the snow globe his mother had sent him for Christmas when he was eleven—the year she'd left him alone on the station with his father—he shook it. Watched all the pretty flakes swirl before slowly settling.

'I can't in good faith… The thing is, poor old Carnelian had a run-in with a barbed-wire fence and his breeding days are over. Now, if you still want him, that can be arranged, but I suspect you're not looking for a pet.'

'Hell, Rose.' He set the globe down with a clatter. 'I'm sorry.'

'Yeah, it sucks.'

He doubted Holt would've been so honest. His father sure as hell wouldn't have been.

It's only fair you get first right of refusal. I can't in good faith...

'Honour is a big thing for you, huh?'

She scowled. 'Yes.'

It made him laugh.

Her scowl only deepened. 'Is it for you?'

He nodded, but said aloud what he knew they both were thinking. 'Except you're a Waverly and I'm a Garrison and we don't trust each other.'

Her sigh sounded loud on the air, but she shook herself upright. 'Which is why my sisters, their husbands, as well as my head stockman, all know where I am and what time I'm expected back. If I'm not back by that time, they'll send out a search party.'

He tried to hide his shock. 'You think I'd kidnap you?'

'I only have three months to fulfil the conditions of the will...and this is a big country.' Her eyes started to dance. 'It's also true that I might be a little bit addicted to soap operas.'

Soap operas? He choked back a laugh.

She leaned towards him, a frown pleating her brow. 'I know we've not spent a lot of time together, Lincoln, but I've known you all my life…'

He waited, his chest growing tighter with each passing second.

'What I do know of you, I like.'

It was as if someone had cut the strings of a puppet—his insides sagged, his heart though took flight.

She stared back, half defiantly. 'I've never seen you be mean to anyone.'

With every word she spoke he fell a little deeper for her. But was it real? Or had he built Rose up in his mind because she was the one that had got away?

His hands clenched and unclenched. He'd always wanted a chance with this woman.

'You're well liked in the district. That's a good character reference.'

'So are you.'

'I'm considered reserved and standoffish.'

Ah, the ice queen tag had reached her ears, then.

'You're well respected,' he said quietly. 'Your judgement is considered as sound as your father's.'

She flinched at the mention of her father. He wished he could hug her.

You could hug her if you were married.

Oh, he was going to marry her, all right, there was no doubt about that.

Glancing at her watch, she shot to her feet. 'Look, I understand this is a lot to take in and that you'll need time to consider your decision. I'm afraid I can only give you a week, though. I've left this far too late and for my family's sake I—'

'If we married…'

He gestured for her to sit. She sat.

'I'd want to maintain the appearance of an actual marriage. I'd want people to think it real.'

'Why?'

'My father is going to be a…challenge. Him thinking the marriage is real will help me manage that.' And that was all he was going to say on the subject.

She chewed that over for a moment. 'You'd have to move to Garrison Downs.'

He nodded.

She nodded too. Not in agreement, but digesting his words. 'It's a moot point until you come to a decision.' She stood again. 'It was good of you to see me at such short notice, and—'

'I'll marry you on one condition, Rose.' He stood too.

Her hands twisted together. 'What's your condition?'

'That for the duration of our marriage, you don't break our wedding vows.'

She blinked. 'You're talking about fidelity.'

'No man likes to be made a fool. I'd promise the same thing. It wouldn't be fair otherwise.'

She gaped at him. 'Lincoln, you're not exactly known for your…abstinence.'

It stung that she thought him incapable of it.

She straightened, her hands on her hips. 'I won't lie to my sisters, and they'll keep the secret if I ask it of them. Other than that, I agree to all of your terms.'

Moving around the desk, he stuck out his hand. 'Deal.'

She clasped it, her grip firm. 'Deal.'

Leaning down, he pressed his lips to her cheek, inhaled her surprisingly light floral scent. 'A pleasure doing business with you, Rose.'

Her breath hitched. 'Likewise.'

She tugged her hand from his with more haste than necessary, and he bit back a grin. Did she really think they'd be able to keep their hands off each other for the next three months? He suspected a paper marriage was the last thing either of them wanted.

CHAPTER TWO

EVE AND NATE were waiting for Rose on her return.

The strange pulse pounding in her throat made it hard to breathe. The touch of Lincoln's lips still burned against her cheek.

Eve searched her face. 'How did it go?'

'Mission accomplished.' Dusting off her hands, she turned to Nate. 'Could we get a wriggle on with this? Organise a special licence?' Because the sooner this was done, the sooner Garrison Downs would be safe. Maybe then she'd breathe easier.

'How soon are you hoping for?'

She knew the norm was a month, but... 'Two weeks?'

The air whistled between his teeth but he gave a slow nod. 'Given where we are, the distances involved, the fact muster will start soon and the responsibilities you and Linc both have... We can make a good case.'

'Excellent.'

Evie grabbed her arm. 'Boss, are you sure about this?'

'I am, I promise.' She squeezed her sister's hand. 'Now, as you know, it's nearly autumn—'

'Which is the busiest time of the year.'

Rose strode off to get changed, but called back over her shoulder, 'The skirt was a great idea, by the way. I think Lincoln is a leg man.'

'Get back here right now and tell me *everything*!'

'Gotta go, Bambi.'

With a grin, she kept walking. She'd do everything in her power to ensure her sisters didn't think she was worried about marrying Lincoln. She had no reason to be worried. She'd wanted him to say yes. He'd said yes. It was all going exactly to plan.

Lincoln's image rose in her mind, the way he'd looked at her, the expression in those dark eyes… the touch of his lips.

She waved a hand in front of her face. Lincoln might be an incredibly attractive man, but there was too much at stake for her to indulge in idle fantasies about him. She'd secure Garrison Downs' future, and do what she could to bring an end to the enmity between their two families. She wasn't letting hormones interfere with that.

Thankfully muster would start soon and she'd be way too busy to think about anything else. But for the first time in a long time, she considered the parts of her life that she'd ignored and neglected for the sake of Garrison Downs and her role here. A familiar burning itched through her. A fire Lincoln had lit seven years ago when, knee deep in mud, their clothes ruined, they'd kissed—

She cut the thought dead. She and Lincoln were different people now. For God's sake, his last girlfriend had been a model—the face of one of Australia's leading cosmetic companies! A man like him wouldn't look at a woman like her twice, and she had no intention of making a fool of herself pining for someone so far out of her league.

God, she was having enough trouble running the station without buying more trouble. Work. That was what she'd focus on. Nothing more.

While Rose was getting ready for bed that evening, her phone rang. She pressed the receiver to her ear. 'Hello?'

'Hello, Rose.'

Lincoln. His voice sounded like a promise and all of the fine hairs on her arms lifted. 'Hello, Lincoln.'

'I have questions.'

She curled up in the chair in her bedroom. 'Fire away.'

'What's your favourite snack?'

It startled a laugh from her. 'Snack?'

'I'm a big chip man myself. If you give me a bag of potato chips I'll hoover them back in record time.'

'Favourite flavour?'

'Salt and vinegar.'

She made a note to stock up. 'My weakness is ice cream. Any flavour. All the flavours. And if a new flavour comes onto the market, I have to try it.'

'When did you last eat a bowl of the good stuff?'

She blinked. She couldn't remember. 'Not for a while.'

'That's too bad. You should always take the time to eat a bowl of ice cream, Rose. It's the little things.'

She found herself suddenly and insanely hungry for ice cream.

'Next question: when are we actually getting married?'

She shook herself. 'In two weeks' time, hopefully. I'll keep you posted.'

'Registry office in Adelaide?'

'That's the plan.' She frowned. 'Unless—'

'Nope, that's fine with me.'

'Okay.' She eased out a breath. 'That brings me to a question of my own.' Shooting to her feet, she strode across to the French doors and pushed outside to the back veranda and the cool night air.

'Which is?'

She grimaced at the night sky—deep and dark and dusted with a thousand stars. 'How are you going to juggle your responsibilities at Kalku while you're living at Garrison Downs?' Lincoln might spend half the year gallivanting around the countryside doing playboy things, but he always returned to help out during muster. When he was home, he worked as hard as the rest of them.

Kalku Hills was nearly as large as Garrison Downs. Under Holt, though, the Waverly holdings had prospered and flourished in a way Kalku Hills had never been able to match. Whatever else she thought of her father, Holt had known cattle and had a deep understanding of the land.

He'd also had an unrivalled business brain, had known how to broker deals and seize opportunities. Under Holt's stewardship, Garrison Downs had become one of the most successful stations in the country. And she had to find a way not only to maintain that legacy, but to carry it on—to continue the expansion, the innovation…the profits.

Weight slammed down on her shoulders. How on earth could she—?

'You've got this, Boss. You know what you're doing.'

She waved a hand in front of her face to dispel her father's voice—*I'm not talking to you!*—dragged her mind back to the matter in hand. 'We can find ways to negotiate it,' she offered. Both stations had planes. Commuting would be involved.

'There's nothing to negotiate. My father fired me this afternoon.'

She digested that in silence. 'Okay.' She kept her voice matter-of-fact. 'If we're going to marry we need to speak plainly, agreed?'

'We promise honesty, Rose, or we call it off here and now. Otherwise there's no point. You want to create a strong working relationship going forward, yes? The only way that's going to happen is if we can learn to trust one another.'

He was right. 'Honesty,' she agreed. 'So with that in mind… Rumour has it that when you're home your father fires you every other day. Now, I expect that's a wild exaggeration, but there's probably a grain of truth in there somewhere.'

'Ah, but the difference is that today I chose to believe him.'

He sounded remarkably cheerful about it. She grimaced. 'He fired you because you told him you're marrying me.'

'He fired me because he's making some truly stupid business decisions, and I challenged him about them.'

He spoke calmly, without anger or rancour. But a memory rose in her mind. She'd been eight years old and in the general store at Marni—the nearest town for a hundred and fifty kilometres. She'd been idly perusing the horse blankets, wondering if she could talk Dad into buying her a flash blue and orange one, when she'd rounded the top of the next aisle—work boots stretched on one side, swags and camping equipment on the other. There'd been bedrolls, camp kettles, enamel plates and mugs. At the other end of the aisle eleven-year-old Lincoln had stood with his father, Clay.

Clay's hand had been raised. It had come crashing down on his son's shoulder with a force that had made her flinch. 'Read it!' As he'd shoved a price tag under his son's nose, that big broad hand had lifted again. 'I said read it!'

Trembling, Rose had reached out a foot and knocked one of the shiny cook pots off the shelf. It had clattered to the floor with a crash, rocking back and forth with a tinny racket. Both father and son had swung around.

Planting her feet, she'd glared at the older man. Lincoln might not know his numbers, but he didn't deserve to be hit like that!

And then Dad had been standing behind her, one hand on her shoulder. With an oath, Clay had stormed off. 'Okay, Linc?' Dad had said.

Lincoln had nodded, then he'd turned and disappeared and the tightness in her chest had slowly eased.

Her father had squeezed her shoulder. 'I'm proud of you, Boss.'

She'd felt good then, until she'd wondered who'd been proud of Lincoln.

'You still there, Rose?'

With a start, she realised her cheeks were wet. She wiped her hands across them. Not long after that incident word had gone around that Lincoln had dyslexia and some kind of hearing issue that had required surgery.

'I'm here.' She recalled the open-handed blow delivered to a young boy's shoulder and her hand clenched around the phone so hard her fingers started to ache. 'I guess he was never going to take the news well.'

'Telling him I was marrying you was simply the icing on the cake.'

The grin in his voice had her biting back a grin of her own. It took an effort to keep her voice steady and level. 'Would you like to come and stay at Garrison Downs early?'

'He isn't kicking me out into the cold, cold snow. I'm not homeless.'

'Never said you were, but your father has a bad temper and I expect he's not that pleasant to be around at the moment.'

Silence greeted her words, and she winced. Had she gone too far?

'I can hold my own.' The words were uttered quietly enough, but steel threaded beneath them.

She nodded. 'I don't doubt that for a moment.' If it were anyone else giving him a hard time, she wouldn't worry, but it was different when it was family. 'That, however, wasn't the question I asked. I asked if you wanted to come and stay at Garrison Downs. It doesn't need to be here at the house. There's a vacant stockman's cottage at the outstation at the moment.'

Walking back into her bedroom, she closed the French doors and leaned against them, stared at the bed. The thought of Lincoln here in her house…

He's going to be in your house, not your bed.

She pushed away from the doors, wrapped common-sense practicality around her like a cloak. 'Lincoln, you know what it's like at this time of year. We're ramping up for muster. You and your Cessna would come in real handy here.'

With the inheritance left to him by his grandfather, Lincoln had bought a racehorse. It had won a lot of races. The prize money had funded the plane and his playboy lifestyle.

'Are you trying to poach me?'

'You're the best in the business. I'd be a fool not to. Anyway, it's not poaching if you're between jobs. I can offer you a contract position for the autumn.' That way he'd be his own boss. 'You can set your own rates.'

Even if he charged twice the going rate, he'd be worth every penny.

'I'll admit I'd like a first-hand look at how you run your operation. Would that bother you?'

'Nope.' He might not hold the reins at Kalku Hills yet, but one day the station would be his. And even if he decided to fritter his time away on inane things—like parties on yachts and movie premieres—he'd hire someone who'd do a better job than his father.

'Is there anyone staying in the cottage out at Ned's Gorge?'

'Nope.'

'Then you have yourself a deal.'

She laughed. 'And here I was thinking the day couldn't get any better.'

'You should do that more. Laugh,' he added before she could ask. 'Are you in bed?'

She climbed beneath the covers. 'Yep. You know we keep early hours out here.'

'Then I'll wish you sweet dreams in just a moment. But first… Will you wear a dress to our wedding?'

An odd note had entered his voice and she blinked. He sounded almost…*vulnerable*. She shook the thought away. 'You want me to wear a dress?'

'More than life itself.'

The words were threaded with a sultry heat and a slow burn started up at the centre of her. Lincoln wanted to see her in a dress? He'd thought about her in a—

'As you so rarely wear dresses, it'll make things look more convincing.'

She crashed back.

'It'll give the ceremony…gravitas.'

He was right. She rarely wore dresses, preferring trouser suits for more formal occasions. She was careful to keep her voice even and crisp. This was business, nothing more. 'Long or short?'

'I don't mind. Just wear something that makes you feel pretty.'

She blinked again. Reminded herself *again* that he didn't mean anything by it.

'What would you like me to wear?'

And she found herself laughing again. He really was every bit the charming shallow playboy the tabloids made him out to be. 'Whatever you think will give the best impression.'

'Sweet dreams, Rose. I'll look forward to speaking to you again soon.'

She suspected her dreams were going to be anything but sweet. 'Goodnight, Lincoln.'

A dress she felt pretty in?

Leaping out of bed, she fired up her laptop to check out her favourite online shops. She wouldn't choose anything too fussy. But she was seized with a sudden desire to make him see her as a woman—just for a few short hours. An attractive and sensual woman, rather than some unsophisticated backwater cow hick.

The next day, when a delivery of rocky road ice cream was flown in from Marni, she laughed. That evening she ate a huge bowlful, enjoying every luscious mouthful.

Lincoln rang her every few days. Always at night as she was getting ready for bed. It became a thing. Sometimes he simply rang to say goodnight. Other nights, if she wasn't dead on her feet, they'd chat longer.

'Tell me something about yourself that I wouldn't know.'

'I'm addicted to *The Bold and the Beautiful*.'

His laugh, all rich warm caramel, made her crave something sweet. 'So that's the soap opera you meant when you mentioned being addicted?'

'One of them. Your turn.'

'I'm good at cricket…'

'That's not a secret.' He'd been the star at the district's annual cricket match for the last decade.

'Ah, but what you wouldn't know is that I'm just as good at chess.'

No way. He didn't seem *serious* enough to play chess.

'You still there, Rose?'

She shook herself, channelled mock outrage. 'Are you challenging me to a game of chess?'

'Rumour has it you're the best in the district. And I can't resist a challenge.'

Said with typical male arrogance. 'I'll look forward to it. I don't play for money, though. Unlike Louisa May and Cordelia, we won't be wagering the station.'

'I'm sure we can think up stakes that are more interesting than that.'

Her eyes narrowed. Had he meant that to sound suggestive?

'Now tell me something else.'

She thought for a moment. 'I call Evelyn Evie, and Matilda Tilly.' She hesitated. Not because she was ashamed or embarrassed, but because it was still so new. 'And I call Anastasia Ana. But nobody calls me Rosie because I hate it.'

'Lots of people call you Boss, as that's what your dad called you.'

She could've hugged him for not peppering her with questions about Ana.

'I'm not going to call you Boss and I won't call you Rosie either. Rose is a beautiful name and it suits you perfectly.'

A funny lump lodged in her throat. 'Do you prefer Linc or Lincoln?'

'Everyone calls me Linc, but you've always called me Lincoln. I like it.'

So did she.

'Next... Do you mind if I hire a photographer to take a few tasteful shots for the press release announcing our marriage?'

Closing her eyes, she grimaced.

'A shot of us exchanging vows, emerging from the registry office married. And then maybe a snap or two of us celebrating at some swish establishment that evening.'

Her eyes snapped open. 'We're spending *the night in Adelaide*?' Her voice rose. What the hell...?

'Rose,' he said gently, 'it's supposed to be our wedding night.'

Damn. She should've seen this coming. The only request Lincoln had made of her was for her to maintain the pretence that this marriage was real. That meant toeing these kinds of lines, playing these kinds of games.

'These aren't going to be tabloid-style shots.'

She tried to unlock her mouth to say okay, but her jaw remained stubbornly clenched.

'And obviously we won't be sharing a room. I'll book two rooms.'

Her jaw promptly released. 'I should've thought of all this myself. But yes, the photographer...a night in Adelaide...fine.'

She heard him move. Was he in bed too? Or maybe out on the porch of the cottage staring up at the stars. She opened her mouth to ask, then closed it. It seemed too personal.

'Are you inviting anyone to the wedding?'

She snuggled down under the covers. 'Just Eve and Nate. You?'

'My father.'

She scowled at the ceiling.

'I haven't spoken to him since I left Kalku, but it only seems right to give him the chance to be there.'

She hoped for Lincoln's sake that Clay showed up to support his son. 'Do you ever see your mother?' Cynthia Garrison had left Clay and Kalku Hills when Lincoln was eleven.

'Once in a blue moon. She's remarried, has

a new family. I'm part of a mistake she wishes she'd never made.'

'You're not a mistake, Lincoln.' Though he'd certainly drawn the short straw as far as family went. No wonder he sought approval and appreciation elsewhere, found it so hard to settle down. 'Don't let your parents make you feel bad for the mistakes they made.'

He was quiet for a moment. 'You'll probably miss your mum on the day.'

Her eyes burned. Her mother would be appalled at Rose marrying for such pragmatic reasons.

'I liked your mother. She was beautiful, classy, elegant. You're a lot like her.'

Her head rocked back. No, she wasn't! Eve and Matilda had Rosamund's beauty and elegance, not Rose. Beside her mother, she'd always felt rough and coarse.

'You must miss her.'

'Every single day.' Her mother had died of pancreatic cancer seven years ago. Even now the speed of it sickened her. Six weeks from diagnosis to death. Not that Rosamund had told them about her diagnosis. She'd kept that to herself. They'd only found it out after she'd collapsed. Everything had changed in the blink of an eye and none of them had been the same since.

'Your mother was always kind to me, always

went out of her way to make me feel welcome. You do the same, Rose. It matters. It means a lot.'

A lump lodged in her throat, making it impossible to speak.

'You still there?'

With a superhuman effort, she dislodged it. 'I wish she could be at my wedding and I wish you'd had the chance to know her better. But I'll have one of my sisters there.' And that meant everything.

'Did you know there's supposed to be a diary of Cordelia's hidden somewhere at Garrison Downs?' he asked one night a few days later.

Rose sat upright in bed. 'A diary?'

'Yeah, my great-grandma told me about it.'

It probably contained a rant or ten about Louisa May and an itemised account of all Waverly offences and shortcomings. Though, one didn't lie in their own diary, did they? Perhaps it revealed how Cordelia had come to lose Garrison Downs in such a reckless fashion?

That poker game between the two women had gained legendary status. Cordelia Garrison wagering a cattle station in a game of cards against Louisa May at the beginning of the last century and losing it. The ensuing scandal and uproar reverberating down the generations.

If they found the diary and discovered the truth… It could help lay old ghosts to rest.

'Or it could make them worse.'

Her grandmother's strident outrage whipped through her, making her flinch.

Oh, right, like I'm going to listen to you, Grandma.

'It's probably long since been lost or destroyed,' Lincoln said.

'I can say with hand on my heart that nothing like that has ever been found.' Or if it had, she'd never been let in on the secret.

'It'd be something to find it though, wouldn't it?'

Something in his voice made her smile. 'A treasure hunt?' She tapped a finger against her chin. 'Old House is probably the best bet.' Old House was the original station homestead. 'Eve and Nate have set up house there. I'll mention it to them, tell them to keep an eye out.'

The night before the wedding, Rose and her sisters gathered for celebratory drinks in Holt's office. She avoided the room whenever she could, refused to work in it, but it was the room with the technology, so...

Tilly in Chaleur appeared on the giant screen soon followed by Ana in Melbourne. Her sisters exchanged surreptitious glances and, from her seat on a pile of cushions that she and Evie had thrown on the floor, Rose rolled her eyes. 'Okay, girls, gather round.'

Everyone leaned closer.

'You know why I'm marrying Lincoln. You know it's a marriage in name only. But I also want you to know that I don't regret doing this, not for a moment. I'd do a whole lot more to safeguard the Downs' future. I just want us clear on that.'

Tilly and Evie exchanged raised eyebrows.

'Now, before the two of you pile in I want to mention a couple of things.'

Tilly pursed her lips. Evie folded her arms. Ana watched, her gaze serious.

'First up, Lincoln signed the prenup without a murmur of complaint.' He wasn't entitled to any part of Garrison Downs beyond Camels Bridge, just as she wasn't entitled to any part of Kalku Hills.

'That's…heartening,' Ana offered.

Rose shot her a smile. 'He hasn't raised any red flags—it's a tick in his favour. The other thing I want to say is that I've always wanted the two stations to work together rather than pulling in separate directions. It's insane for us to be at constant loggerheads. It'd save both stations a lot of time and money if we could work cooperatively. Holt would never see sense on the subject.' She ground her teeth together. 'Frankly, the way he and Clay have acted over the years is disgraceful.'

Tilly's jaw dropped. 'Rose!'

She blinked. 'What? I didn't agree with him about everything.'

'I know, but when the two of you argued you never sounded like…*that*.'

'Like what?'

'Furious,' Eve supplied.

Tilly nodded. 'You worshipped the ground Dad walked on.'

Once maybe, but… She hadn't spoken to them about it. The last nine months had been hell, and the time had never felt right. 'I *am* furious.' She grew tense with that fury all over again. 'I'm *never* going to forgive him for keeping Ana from us.'

'Oh, Rose.' Ana's bottom lip wobbled.

She retied her ponytail. 'That's a discussion for another day. The fact is Holt was brilliant in a lot of ways, but he could be a jerk at times too. He enjoyed playing top dog in the district, and he loved rubbing Clay's face in it.'

'Clay isn't a very nice man, though,' Tilly murmured.

'Agreed. But going forward I think Lincoln and I can forge a stronger working relationship between the two stations. It's beyond time the bad blood between our families came to an end.'

'Hear, hear.' But Evie's brow pleated. 'Can you trust him, though?'

Rose's heart sounded loud in her ears in the sudden hush of the room.

Tilly stared at her. 'What do your instincts tell you?'

Both Tilly and Evie leaned towards her. Rose

pressed her fingers together and swallowed. 'Lincoln might refuse to live his life seriously, he might bounce from woman to woman, but he's *not* his father. I believe he can be trusted.'

Both her sisters sagged in relief. Evie glanced up at Ana. 'Rose's judgement is practically infallible.'

Rose's stomach gave a sick kick. Dear God, if it let her down this time… Swallowing her doubts, she forced up her chin. 'Hey, here's something. Lincoln's great-grandma told him that Cordelia's diary is supposed to be hidden somewhere at the Downs.'

'Ooh!' Tilly clasped her hands beneath her chin. 'How wonderful if we could find it.' As an historian and a graphologist who was called upon to give advice about the authenticity of old letters, this was totally Tilly's jam.

'I reckon Old House is our best bet,' Rose said.

'Oh, my God! Nate and I will tear the house apart. If it's there, we'll find it.'

The women talked for a little longer before signing off and promising to talk again soon. Both Tilly and Ana wished Rose well for the following day.

But as Rose readied herself for bed that night, thoughts of Cordelia's diary circled through her mind. The enmity between the Waverlys and the Garrisons had an origin, even if that origin was now shrouded in hearsay and speculation. She understood, even sympathised, with everyone's excitement and curiosity, but a part of her couldn't help wondering if finding that diary would open a whole other can of worms that would be better off remaining buried.

CHAPTER THREE

LINCOLN CHOSE TO believe that the unhindered sun that dawned on the day of his wedding was a good omen. Rose wore a dress in a shade of deep dusky pink that matched her name, the material caressing her curves with a loving attention that had his mouth going dry. He couldn't believe he was going to marry this woman.

His father didn't show. Rose glanced around, but didn't say anything, just reached up to trace a finger down his tie—pale blue silk, covered in a print of pink tea roses. He shrugged. 'Made me think of you.'

Curling her hand in the crock of his arm, she turned them in the direction of the reception desk. 'Let's go do this.'

The service was fast and efficient—'i's dotted and 't's crossed. Before they knew it, they were standing blinking in the sun again. Rose glanced up and her lips twitched. 'Here's to the beginning of a beautiful friendship.'

He sent her a lazy grin. 'Ah, Rose, we'll always have Adelaide.' That twitch blossomed into a full-blown smile, and hope burned a path through his chest. 'I made a lunch reservation at the Grand Hotel in Glenelg.'

Eve gave a delighted squeak.

'And booked two ocean-view suites for the night.' The views of the Southern Indian Ocean from the hotel were stunning.

Rose's smile faded. He maintained a deliberately cheerful manner, refusing to let thoughts of his playboy reputation mar the day. She might doubt his intentions, but he planned on being the perfect gentleman.

Seducing Rose would only reinforce her view of him. He needed to take things slow. Call him a sentimental fool, but he actually wanted her to like him before they embarked on a sexual relationship. *If* they embarked on a sexual relationship. He refused to take anything for granted.

'You deserve a night away from the station, Boss. It'll do you good.' Eve folded her arms. 'You ought to make it two.'

Rose shook her head. 'There's too much to do.'

'An extra night wouldn't make any difference… except giving you a bit of a break.'

Eve was worried that Rose was working too hard?

'Besides, you and Lincoln must have things you want to discuss away from prying eyes. You can give me the orders for the rest of the week and I'll make sure Aaron gets them.'

'Aaron knows what needs doing for the next few days.'

'Yeah, but will he do it?' Eve muttered. 'I heard you arguing with him again the other day.'

Rose was having trouble with her head stockman?

'Evie, one night away is more than enough.'

He thought of his father then and nodded. 'It is.' He clapped his hands. 'The plan. Tonight I thought dinner at a waterfront restaurant that does an amazing seafood platter. After that...' He shrugged. 'We were both up at the crack of dawn so I can't see us dancing into the wee small hours, but... Do you like whisky, Rose? There's supposed to be a speakeasy somewhere close by that does tastings. I thought it might be fun.'

She glanced up, moistened her lips. 'Dinner, followed by the speakeasy and then a relatively early night sounds good to me.'

'And then home tomorrow?'

'Perfect.'

And he made sure it was. He kept her laughing, made sure the conversation flowed, and didn't make a single inappropriate move. As he fell into bed at midnight, he couldn't remember the last time he'd enjoyed himself more.

Eve met them on their return the next day. Linc swooped down, lifting Rose into his arms before they could step inside the homestead.

Startled blue eyes blinked into his. 'What are you doing?'

Was it his imagination or was her voice a fraction high? He might want to take things slow, but it didn't mean he didn't want her aware of him. 'I believe it's traditional for the groom to carry the bride across the threshold, Mrs Waverly.' He'd taken for granted that she'd keep her own name, but as to the title... 'Do you want to be a Mrs, or would you rather remain a Ms?'

'I think, perhaps, I'd rather you put me down before you dropped me.'

'I'm not going to drop you.' He grinned, loving the feel of her in his arms. 'I'll be happy to hold you all day until you decided the Ms or Mrs question.' He manoeuvred through the doorway with care. And then just stood there, patiently waiting.

At least, he hoped he looked patient. An armful of warm delicious woman had everything starting to throb. 'Don't you worry about me, Rose.' He widened his smile. 'Like I said, I could do this all day and not break out in a sweat.'

'Okay, okay. *Mrs* Waverly, all right? It'll keep the lawyers happy.'

'Perfect.' Reluctantly he set her on her feet.

When he straightened, he found Eve biting her lip as if trying not to laugh. 'Refreshment time!' She linked arms with Rose and led the way through to the kitchen.

The homestead was luxurious—a series of spacious elegant rooms with large creamy interiors and dark antiques—graceful and classic. It dazzled and charmed in equal measure.

'You should be taking it easy, Evie.'

'Morning tea with my sister and her new husband, especially when neither Lindy nor Nate will let me lift a finger, doesn't count as hard labour. It *is* me taking it easy.'

Which made Rose laugh. And that made him smile. The sisters' closeness fascinated him. As a boy, he'd watched Rose and her family on race days and show days, hungry for what they had, wondering what it'd be like if he had a brother or sister.

'Lincoln, this is our housekeeper, Lindy.'

A dark-haired woman, probably a decade older than Rose and half a head shorter, glanced up from the jug she was filling with ice cubes. 'Welcome to Garrison Downs, Mr Garrison.'

'Linc,' he automatically corrected.

'Many congratulations to both of you on your marriage.'

'Thanks, Lindy, much appreciated.'

'Lindy's homemade lemonade is to die for,' Eve said.

Rose nodded. 'And her date scones.'

He filed all of it away.

That evening Linc strolled into the living room to find Rose curled up on the sofa with a pile of paperwork. River, Holt's retired border collie, dozed on the floor nearby. Rose glanced up as he set a neatly wrapped package on the coffee table in front of her. 'I bought you a wedding present.'

River stood to sniff it. Lincoln ruffled the border collie's ears. He'd ordered this present two weeks ago, after getting off the phone to Rose that first night.

She set the paperwork to one side. 'You didn't have to do that.'

'I wanted to.'

'I...uh...have something for you, too, but you'll have to wait until tomorrow. We ran out of time for me to show it to you today.'

They hadn't, but he didn't challenge her. After morning tea with Eve and Nate, Rose had given him a comprehensive tour of the house—which hadn't included a peek inside her bedroom, but she'd touched the door as they passed to indicate it was hers. She'd placed him in the room next door and had left him to *settle in*, then had disappeared for the rest of the day.

He sat beside her now, close, but not too close. He might not be the playboy she thought him, but nor was he a saint. He wanted her aware of him, unable to ignore him. He leaned in, breathed deeply. 'You smell great.'

'I...uh...it's probably my shampoo.' She edged away a fraction, her tongue snaking out to moisten her lips.

It was still there. The heat between them. It chafed at her in the same way it chafed at him. The knowledge hummed through him. 'Go on.' He nudged her. 'Open it.'

Leaning forward, she tore the paper from the gift. 'A chess set!'

'Ah, but not just any old chess set—a *themed* chess set. A *soap-opera*-themed chess set.'

Pulling it free from its box, she lifted out one of the pieces, her bark of laughter making him grin. 'Where are on earth did you find it?'

'You can find anything on the Internet these days.' Not quite true. He'd had this one specially made.

She turned the piece over in her fingers—a baron masquerading as a moustache-twirling villain. 'This is amazing, Lincoln. I love it!'

He'd known she would. 'Wanna play a game?'

She hesitated.

'You can tell a lot about a person by the way they accept defeat.' He seized a king—a smug tycoon wearing a Stetson and holding a fistful of dollars. 'And I'm looking forward to seeing your face when I trounce you.'

She placed a swooning maiden on the board. 'You know I'm going to wipe the floor with you?'

'In your dreams.' With a lazy finger, he touched the tiger eye set into the bracelet she wore. She'd worn it the day she'd proposed. She'd worn it yesterday, too. 'This is pretty.'

She stilled. 'Ana had one made for each of us. They're all set with a different stone. She calls them sister bracelets.'

The tiger eye suited her. 'What's Ana like?' He kept setting up, not wanting to make a big deal of his question.

'Incredibly talented. Smart. Strong.' The words were short and clipped. 'Why?'

He fought an urge to close his eyes. Despite everything, he was still a Garrison. And she a Waverly. Trust wasn't part of their DNA.

Pushing an ottoman across to the other side of the coffee table, he sat down on it and folded his arms too. 'I envied you all when I was growing up, did you know that? I wished my parents had given me a brother or sister before their marriage imploded.'

Something in her face softened. 'I'm sorry. I shouldn't have snapped. I'm just sick of the gossip.'

He nodded.

She kept setting up the board, not meeting his eye. 'Sisters are the best. And Ana is a sister. She's one of us.'

It was enough. For now. 'Okay, game on. You be white.'

Rose found it ridiculously difficult to concentrate on chess. Lincoln wasn't doing anything exceptional. He wasn't flirting. But she was minutely aware of him. When he'd leaned in earlier to sniff her, gooseflesh had broken out on her arms. It had taken a superhuman effort not to chafe them away.

She glanced at him, glanced back at the board. Of course he wasn't flirting. She'd made it clear she wanted a marriage in name only. And she was well aware that a woman like her had nothing to tempt a man like him. If only that worked in reverse.

Gritting her teeth, she told herself this was nothing but a mixture of nerves and relief. Tomorrow she could bury herself in work and everything would return to normal again.

Seizing one of her pieces, she moved it. 'Pawn to Queen Four.'

He responded with, 'Pawn to King Three.'

Her brows shot up.

He winked at her and it made her chest catch. 'Didn't think I'd know the lingo?'

'Sorry, I used it without thinking. It's not the way they call games any more, but it's the way Pop taught me.'

They played in silence, but every time she glanced up she found those dark eyes watching her. Once she swore she saw heat in their depths. It made her blood leap.

Don't be stupid!

But the long-ago memory of Lincoln ringing to invite her to dinner lifted through her. Things had leapt inside her then too, and she'd had to clench her eyes shut to dispel the image of the way his eyes had flared before their one and only kiss. She'd wanted to say yes so much it had hurt. She hadn't. She'd said, 'Lincoln, we can't go on a date. I can't hurt my family like that.'

'It's *just one date*, Rose,' had been his reply and she'd felt like an idiot then, because it had felt like so much more. But it wasn't. It was *just one date*.

His words had snapped her out of foolish daydreams, had her pulling herself back into straight lines. 'Thank you for the invitation, but I don't have time for dating at the moment. Please don't ask me again.'

It hadn't been a lie. After her mother's recent death, her father had needed her in ways he never had before. She'd refused to add to his pain—his consuming grief.

She'd been proven right in not dating Lincoln, though. He'd gone on to date *so many* women. She'd have just been one in a long line. He'd have broken her inexperienced heart. And she'd have hurt her family for nothing. For heaven's sake, even now whenever she saw his picture in the newspaper, some beautiful woman on his arm, it sent a sting through her.

Glancing up, she found a frown in those bitter chocolate eyes. 'Where did you just go?' His face gentled. 'You looked so sad.'

Lincoln might have the attention span of a flea

when it came to women but it didn't change the fact that he was kind. And her heart was still every bit as inexperienced now as it had been seven years ago. She couldn't misinterpret that kindness. She needed to be careful. Before she could come up with a reply, Lindy appeared in the doorway.

'Linc, a delivery just arrived for you.'

Lincoln stood with his familiar indolence. 'I sent some things on to Marni from Kalku. Was going to borrow a vehicle and collect them tomorrow. Someone must've sent them on.'

'That's uh, not what this is. It's a…special delivery from your father.'

Clay hadn't shown up at the registry office yesterday. This could be an olive branch. Or it could be mischief. Rose stood too, and prayed for Lincoln's sake that it was the former.

Reaching into the corridor outside, Lindy brought forth a small animal carrier. Inside was an ugly marmalade tabby. Rose had a sudden image of her mother sitting in Holt's office with an elegant chocolate and cream shorthair on her lap, stroking its fur and cooing softly.

She raised an eyebrow in Lincoln's direction, but he was already striding across to take possession of the crate. 'Thanks, Lindy.' Walking back, he set it on the ottoman. Kneeling down he said, 'Hey there, Colin. How you doing, buddy?'

A loud purring immediately filled the air.

Mischief. Definitely mischief. 'Why would your father send you a cat?' She did her best to keep her voice neutral.

'How do you feel about cats, Rose?'

Not enthusiastic. Not when they had working dogs. Not with dingoes around. Damn it, cats could do a lot of damage to the native wildlife, were a disaster if they went feral. All farmers knew that.

He grimaced at whatever he saw in her face.

'Tell me he's microchipped, registered and de-sexed.'

'He is.'

'He'll have to be an inside cat.'

'Absolutely.' He glanced across the room. 'How's River with cats?'

'Fine. My mother had a series of shorthair Burmese cats when we were growing up. River came to an understanding with the last one. But…' She gestured at the cat and raised her hands. 'Why?'

One broad shoulder lifted. 'He's a stray I picked up in Adelaide last year. Half starved, half dead. I took him to a vet—not registered or micro-chipped. The vet was going to put him down.' He rolled his shoulders. 'It seemed a bit harsh.'

Oh, God, why did he have to be such a gor-geous big…*marshmallow*?

'My father wasn't a member of the Colin fan club either.'

Hence the reason Colin was now here in her living room.

Biting back a sigh, she moved across to crouch in front of the carrier. 'Hello, Colin, welcome to Garrison Downs. I'd appreciate it if you'd be on your best behaviour for the next couple of days while we get to know one another.'

Easing back, she nodded at Lincoln to let the poor cat out.

When the door opened, Colin's head emerged. He looked as if someone—or something—had chewed off half his ear. The rest of him followed with a regal air at odds with his appearance. Lincoln's lips twitched. She bit back a grin.

Lifting his head, he sniffed the air and then, with an unholy yowl, swung in the direction of River quietly dozing on the other side of the coffee table. River lifted his head, instantly alert. Upon seeing the cat, he stood and shook himself, gave a friendly bark.

A signal Colin clearly misinterpreted as a call to arms as he immediately charged the poor dog. River might be old but he was still nimble. He took off around the room with the cat in hot pursuit.

'Do something,' she yelled at Lincoln.

'Colin! *Stop that!*'

'Very effective.' At her signal River made straight across the room to her, jumping up on the coffee table and scattering the chess pieces in all directions before leaping onto the sofa. Rose moved to shield him and, with one hand held out, hollered, 'Stop!'

Amazingly, Colin did.

'You want back in your crate?' she threatened, pointing at the crate.

Colin sat amid the debris of the coffee table, curled his tail around himself and started cleaning one paw. Lincoln scooped him up, grinning. 'You've a way with him already.'

Rolling her eyes, she glanced behind to find Lindy holding onto the doorway convulsing with laughter. 'I'll get the trays and bowls and whatnot out of storage, shall I?'

'Thanks, Lindy.'

She turned and then tried not to melt at the sight of the big strong man holding the big ugly kitty who clearly adored him. Lincoln stood there looking impossibly wonderful. Impossibly gorgeous. Impossibly out of reach.

He glanced up and froze at whatever he saw in her face.

Oh, God. Had she been making big cow eyes at him?

Very slowly he eased Colin to the floor. Then he ambled across until they stood so close she could see the lighter amber flecks that glinted in his eyes. 'If you ever want to change the terms of our agreement, Rose…'

He was talking about sex. She took a step back, her heart pounding. 'I don't.'

He raised an eyebrow.

Damn it! She couldn't very well deny that she'd been checking him out. 'Look, you're an attractive man, but…no.'

He folded his arms, looking as strong and sturdy as a mountain. 'We're consenting adults. We find each other attractive.'

He found her attractive? Fat chance. She'd probably do as a stopgap. But she didn't want to be anyone's stopgap. Instinct warned her that this man would threaten her peace of mind…and even her heart, if she let him.

And that was out of the question.

'We're not going to dance this particular dance, Lincoln. There's too much at stake. We might both be footloose and fancy-free—'

'Neither of us is footloose and fancy-free.' His eyes flashed. 'For the next three months we're *married*.'

Her heart hammered in her throat. 'I'm not going to break the promises I made you. But you have a reputation. I expect you'll find three months of abstinence…challenging.'

'That's harsh.' One eyebrow cocked. 'Especially in light of the fact that I've not been with a woman in over fourteen months.'

Her jaw dropped. 'But…' That was impossible. 'You've been photographed with eight or nine different women in the last year!'

He sent her a slow grin. 'Been counting, Rose?'

She had. But she wasn't admitting as much.

'I expect it's been a while for you too.'

If she told him she'd never had a lover, would he laugh out loud, run scared, or see it as a challenge? None of those scenarios filled her with enthusiasm.

She fixed him with what she hoped was a glare. 'All I want is for us to be friends. And if that's not possible, then for us to at least not be enemies.'

'I want that too.' The expression in his eyes flattened. 'And just for the record, our relationship won't ever become physical until you like me rather than loathe me.'

'I don't loathe you!'

But she found herself talking to thin air. Lincoln had already marched from the room.

CHAPTER FOUR

LINC LEANED BACK in his chair and sent Rose a slow grin when she strode into the kitchen the next morning. 'You're looking radiant this morning, Rose.' The unguarded hunger he'd surprised in her eyes last night still had him wondering if he ought to be fanning the flames rather than taking things slow.

She startled, glared, and then rolled her eyes at Lindy, and he knew she thought he was flirting for the housekeeper's benefit.

'Looks like we've a morning person in our midst.'

Lindy's chuckle could be heard over the spitting and crackling of bacon. Reaching for a mug with 'Boss' stamped on it, Lindy filled it to the brim with hot dark coffee and pushed it across to Rose, who promptly buried her face in it.

When she surfaced a few moments later, everything about her had sharpened. Coffee, it seemed, was a non-negotiable first thing in the morning. *This.* Hunger and possessiveness shot through him in equal measure. He wanted *this*—to learn everything about Rose; to know her in ways no one else did.

'Thanks, Lindy.' Rose plonked down on the seat across from him.

Lindy placed poached eggs in front of Rose, and bacon and eggs in front of Linc, and a towering plate of toast between them. 'It's nice to have another morning person around. Reminds me of the way it was when Holt was here.'

Rose's face instantly closed.

That expression… He eased back. From where he was sitting, it looked less like grief and more like anger.

Holt had always been larger than life—a walking, talking, living, breathing legend. A man who could do no wrong. The news of his affair must've rocked Rose to her very foundations.

Not a topic he meant to raise today, though. 'What's on for the day?'

'I need to get a report from the outstation, check in with the trucking companies to make sure we're coordinated for the muster. And we have a vet visit at the stud that I want in on. After that it's routine maintenance on the bikes and quads.'

'Where would I be most useful?'

'Tomorrow I'd say out on Judy, checking herd locations, but today there's something I want to show you.'

His ears pricked at something in her voice, at the bright flash of blue in her eyes.

'After that, the choice is yours. It's—'

She broke off, already on her feet when Aaron strode into the kitchen. 'What's wrong? Is anyone hurt?'

Her head stockman shook his head.

Linc didn't stand. He eased his chair back and stretched out his legs. He preferred to conserve his energy—only kicking into action when necessary. And he wanted to assess the dynamics here. Rose had mentioned that Aaron was overseeing the building of the new yard on the central western boundary. Why was he here?

'We have a problem.'

Rose put her hands on her hips. 'Which is?'

Aaron flicked a glance in Lincoln's direction. The dislike in his eyes had Linc's mind whirring, though he was careful to keep his posture deceptively lazy. This was one of the reasons people dismissed him as a lightweight—he gave nothing away. It made them think he wasn't paying attention, wasn't processing what was happening. It had given him an edge more times than he could count.

Aaron's face twisted. 'Cattle have gone missing on the south-eastern boundary.'

The boundary with Kalku Hills? Things inside him tensed. Had his father taken advantage of the fact that both he and Rose had been in Adelaide?

Had he whisked the cattle away while attention was elsewhere? His gut clenched. It was clearly what Aaron thought.

'We're talking over a thousand head of prime—'

'Thank you, Aaron, I'm well aware of the numbers.'

Her face tightened and his chest hollowed.

Blue eyes flashed. 'Why am I hearing this news from you? Why hasn't Nick rung it in to me directly? Why aren't you overseeing the building of the new yard?'

The safety of those yards was a prime concern of every cattleman in the country. If the yards didn't hold, if just one element was overlooked, it could spell disaster.

'It's just as well I am here! I not only—'

'You mean to tell me you never *left*?'

'Johnno is more than capable of overseeing the yard and—'

He doesn't have the experience you do! You had no right—'

She broke off, breathing heavily, glancing at Linc. She moderated her tone, clearly not wanting to upbraid the man in front of him. Probably wise. 'You and I are going to have a serious conversation *very* soon, Aaron. I want you out at that yard now.'

'What about the missing cattle?'

'Lincoln and I will take care of it.'

'Him?'

Aaron's face twisted before he started around the table in Linc's direction. Linc stood in one unhurried motion. If the man threw a punch, he wasn't giving him a height advantage.

Aaron stabbed a finger at him. 'If you hurt her, me and the boys will take you out the back and beat you senseless and leave you for the dingoes.'

'Aaron!' Rose snapped. From the corner of his eyes he saw Lindy cover her mouth.

Linc moved in close to Aaron. Aaron was a big man, but Linc was bigger—taller and broader—and he used all of that now to deliberately loom over the other man, though he was careful to keep a pleasant expression on his face. 'And if you hurt Rose you'll have to answer to me. I won't need anyone else. I'll be enough.'

'All right, enough.' Rose moved between them and pushed them apart.

'You know what the Garrisons are!' Aaron flung out an arm. 'You know they can't be trusted!'

'Careful, Aaron.' Her voice had gone dangerously soft. 'Are you accusing my new husband and my father-in-law of stealing Garrison Downs' cattle?'

She moved in close, deliberately in Aaron's face. She might be half a head shorter, but she bristled all over and it reminded him of the way Colin had charged River last night, smaller but fiercer. 'You need to be very sure before you start throwing accusations like that around.'

She said the words as if by rote. He'd bet she'd learned them at her father's knee.

'You can ruin a good reputation with unfounded accusations, and out here one's reputation is their livelihood. You *know* that.' Reaching up, she grabbed his hat from his head and slapped it against his chest. 'No hats in the house! You know that too. Now go.'

She strode back to the table and seized a piece of toast, bit into it ferociously. Aaron didn't move. She turned back, her eyes narrowing. 'And?'

'Franz Arteta rang. He's put a hold on the contract.'

Her shoulders drew as tight as the strings on a freshly strung tennis racquet.

'And when the Graziers Association rang to ask if you'd give the annual address, I told them you'd be delighted to.' He smirked. 'If you're not up to it, though, I'll do it.'

Lincoln wasn't taking that sitting down. 'Everyone knows you've wanted the association gig for the last five years, mate, but that's not the way to go about getting it. If they'd wanted you, they'd have asked you.'

Aaron turned a dark shade of red.

Ambling around the table, Lincoln rested an arm across Rose's shoulders. 'I've wanted it for the last five years too. Rose, though, will do a brilliant job.'

A shiver swept through her, not visible, but he

felt it. She didn't want to give the annual address? But it was considered an honour. Holt had given the address multiple times and—

Ah... Holt's were ridiculously large shoes to fill. It'd be enough to intimidate anyone.

He kept speaking to give her time to collect herself. 'You know she's the right person, I know it, and more importantly the association knows it.'

Silence stretched through the room. Seizing his orange juice, Lincoln downed it in one go. 'I am, however, the best pilot in the district. Guess I better go get ready. You two probably have other things to discuss.'

'Nope.' Aaron started for the door, clearly realising that if Lincoln left, Rose would give him *what for* in no uncertain terms. 'I'll get out to the new yard now.'

Rose glanced at Lincoln and he waited for her to tell him she didn't need anyone to fight her battles for her. Instead she gestured for him to sit and finish his breakfast. 'That was nicely done. You put him in his place, but placed yourself on his level too.'

'Wouldn't work for you, not when you're the boss.'

He wanted to ask how far Aaron was overstepping. He wanted to know why the association address intimidated her. And who the hell was Franz Arteta and what contract had he put on hold? If he could, he'd fix *all* the things.

'Finish your breakfast, Lincoln, we've a long day ahead of us.'

She spoke as if on automatic pilot, her mind racing behind the blue of her eyes.

'Yes, ma'am.'

She started, her lips hooking up in a reluctant smile. 'The girls always did call me bossy boots. Sorry.'

'Forgiven…on the proviso you sit down and finish your breakfast too.'

She did. When they'd finished up, she stacked their plates in the dishwasher, Lindy having long since moved on to some other chore. 'Lincoln, while you're here I don't want you putting up with any insults—veiled or otherwise. I want that nonsense knocked on its head as soon as it shows its face.'

'I can look after myself, Rose. I keep telling you that.' She opened her mouth, but he got in first. 'No hats in the house, huh?'

'No boots, no hats—my mother's rule.'

He loved the inbuilt continuity and unspoken respect of it. 'I won't forget. Now for this reconnaissance—plane or chopper?'

'The plane would get us there faster, but the chopper will give us more manoeuvrability.'

'Chopper,' they both agreed.

An hour later they were flying across Garrison Downs' southern boundary.

'Rose, I don't know what kind of trash talk Aaron's been indulging in, but the district thinks you're doing a brilliant job.'

He pretended his attention was on the land stretching away beneath them, but from the corner of his eye he saw the way she rocked back in her seat as if his words had shocked her. The way her hands half lifted as if to press against her eyes.

His jaw clenched. *Damn Aaron.* Rose had enough on her plate without him undermining her. 'We both know what Garrison Downs means to the local economy. It's not fair, I know, but people have been watching, waiting, trying to calculate the fallout from the change in circumstances.'

He met her gaze briefly. 'But there hasn't been any. The transition has been seamless. Everyone is impressed with the job you're doing. Seriously impressed.'

Moistening her lips, she nodded. 'Good. Not that they're impressed with me. That's neither here nor there. But that fears have eased. I know…' A breath shuddered out of her. 'I know how worried people have been. I'm glad confidence in Garrison Downs is building again.'

'Holt is a hard act to follow, but you've got what it takes to step into his shoes. You know your land, you know the business, you know the challenges facing the industry. Don't let anyone convince you otherwise. From where I'm sitting, you seem to be doing it with ease—with one arm tied behind your back while standing on your head.'

She huffed out a laugh and he let out a careful breath. Rose had the weight of the world on her shoulders. He'd do whatever he could to lighten her load.

Twenty minutes later they were flying over the area where last week Lincoln had called in his sighting of a large herd. Nothing. Not a steer or heifer in sight. Rose craned her neck to look at the control panel. 'The coordinates are right.'

This was exactly where he'd have expected to find them. 'Want me to check the fence line with Kalku?'

'Yes, please.'

He heard her sigh through the headphones. She had to suspect Clay was behind this. Acid burned his throat. And maybe him.

Not once had she asked him if he thought his father responsible, though. He still hadn't worked out how he'd answer if she did. Would he tell her the truth?

Or would he lie?

Damn it! Fact of the matter was he thought his father as guilty as hell. He should never have invited Clay to the wedding, should never have let him know he'd be away from the station for even a day. He'd been so careful during the last fortnight, making his father aware that he was patrolling the boundary with an eagle eye.

Clay had always believed that Garrison Downs should've been his—that it'd been stolen from him a hundred and twenty years ago—but Linc never had. What Clay refused to see was that he'd have never made a success of the place the way Holt had. That was what really stuck in his father's craw. It was why he hid behind that ancient poker match with its rumours of cheating and foul deeds, bleating about what could've been.

Seizing the binoculars, Rose focussed on something below.

Linc rubbed a hand over his face. How the hell was he going to convince Rose to trust him when—?

'Lincoln, can you take us down?'

He crashed back, stared at the land below. What the hell had she seen?

Rose stared at the tracks made by a quad bike—fresh tracks—and the familiar marks made by a mob of cattle on the move and bit back something rude and succinct.

She couldn't look at Lincoln, afraid her thoughts would show on her face.

'Rose.' Lincoln pointed to a brand-new section of fence—a recent repair. As if it had been cut to allow a herd of cattle to pass though. 'There was nothing wrong with this boundary when I flew over it a few days ago.'

He'd been keeping an eye on their boundary

with Kalku? Had he been scouting for his father? Feeding Kalku the locations of Garrison Down cattle?

Her stomach churned. In marrying Lincoln, had she made the sorriest mistake of her life?

'Hold your horses, Boss. You know—'

Shut up. I'm not talking to you.

'I knew nothing about this, I swear.'

The low throb in his voice burned through her. Stalking over to the fence, she forced herself to assess the ground on the other side, searching for clues. Frowned.

'If my father is behind this—'

She whirled on him. 'We *don't* make unsubstantiated accusations.' She pointed a finger at him. *'Ever.'*

Corded forearms folded across a substantial chest. 'You sounded like Holt then.'

From beneath the wide brim of his hat, his mouthed kinked up and her heart did some dumb lamb-like cavort thing. She forced her gaze away. 'Yeah, well, it was one of the things we did agree on,' she bit out.

The anger she harboured against Holt was getting harder and harder to contain. She needed to get a grip. She didn't want anyone, and certainly not Lincoln, sensing what she refused to say out loud—that there were multiple issues she and Holt hadn't agreed on.

Like hiding a daughter away as if she was something to be ashamed of.

Like not letting her know her sisters.

The injustice of it—the moral bankruptcy—still burned through her as fierce and hot today as it had when Harrington had read the will nine months ago.

Boss—

But that wasn't where her focus should currently be. She turned back to Lincoln. 'Do you remember Roddy Jackson?'

Squinting into the sun, he nodded.

Rumours had started getting around that Roddy, a local grazier, wasn't paying his suppliers. Somehow the rumours had gathered momentum and people began to cross the street so they didn't have to talk to Roddy whenever he went into town. One day he was refused service at the pub.

He'd gone home and had tried to take his own life. Luckily he hadn't succeeded, and it had eventually come to light that his accountant had been cooking the books. Roddy hadn't been responsible at all. It had made a huge impression on her.

It had made a huge impression on Holt, too. Out here a person's reputation was everything.

The hard light in Lincoln's eyes as he stared at the ridge in the distance, and the white line of his mouth, had her swallowing. Maybe he wasn't responsible for this. Maybe he and his father weren't working together to steal her cattle.

We don't make unsubstantiated accusations.

She straightened. She'd take her own advice. She'd keep her eyes and ears open, and judge based on the evidence she saw—*not* hearsay or inherited suspicion.

And what was the current evidence? She breathed out slowly. 'Look at the ground on the other side of the fence, Lincoln.'

He did as she ordered. She had to stop doing that—barking orders at him as if he were some green station hand. Air whistled between his teeth. 'No tracks.'

She folded her arms and rested back against a fence post. 'Not one. The cattle will still be on Garrison Down land somewhere. An experienced cattleman on a quad bike, with a good working dog—' and they all had good working dogs '—could easily cut a thousand head of cattle into five separate herds of two hundred. Or even ten herds of a hundred if he had the time and inclination.'

'My father?'

'Holt and Clay have been at this nonsense since they were teenagers.' A tit-for-tat back-and-forth that passed for sport out here.

Lincoln's jaw clenched. She shrugged. 'I wasn't supposed to know.'

'Why the hell didn't I know too? Where was my head at?'

'Rumour had it your head was always taken up with your latest busty blonde.'

That had him grinning. 'Is that an unsubstantiated rumour?'

'Not if the pictures in the papers are anything to go by.'

Those dark eyes surveyed her as the smile slowly dissolved. 'Just so you know, Rose, they weren't all blonde, nor were they necessarily busty.'

Fourteen months.

He'd not been with a woman for fourteen months. Why had he told her that?

She pushed away from the fence. It didn't matter. It was none of her business. And she *didn't* care. 'Come on, let's go find my missing cattle. Those hills to the north are our best bet.'

CHAPTER FIVE

In March the days were long and warm, but the evenings held a welcome hint of coolness. Rose pulled clean air into her lungs and let it out slowly, her fingers idly ruffling Blossom's fur. Like River, her working dog, Blossom, was a lilac border collie. She'd had her since she was a pup. Unlike River, though, as a working dog she was relegated to the back veranda.

They both enjoyed the early evening stillness, broken only by the 'chet-chet' chattering of a flock of galahs, their feathers flashing pink and grey as they flew in to nest for the night, the horizon softening from a deep orange to muted bands of lilac and blue.

The French doors to Lincoln's room opened to her left. He strode out—freshly showered and wearing a pair of low-slung denims and a white T-shirt. If she were the director of a soap opera, she'd have made that T-shirt ridiculously tight so viewers could appreciate every superb muscle.

Actually, as a director she'd probably have him ditch the shirt altogether.

Oh, for heaven's sake.

Swallowing hard, she forced herself into relaxed lines. 'Evening, Lincoln.'

He turned with that customary indolence. 'I wondered where you'd disappeared to.'

It'd been a fraught day, searching for the scattered cattle, but they could both relax now. The cattle had been found. She gestured at the view. 'I love it out here at this time of day.'

He nodded. 'The gardens here are a real treat. Up for an amble?'

She accepted the hand he held out, let him pull her to her feet. He didn't relinquish her hand, but wrapped his fingers firmly around hers. The bare skin of his arm brushed against the bare skin of her arm. Her throat went so tight it hurt. What did he think he was doing? Gritting her teeth, she tugged her hand from his. Did what she could to ignore the warmth and temptation of the man.

They walked in silence for a bit. 'Rose, are you worried about giving the annual address for the Graziers Association?'

The question took her off guard.

'I get the impression you are, but I don't see why you would be.'

She folded her arms tight across her chest. 'Ooh, let me see… Maybe because they only asked me hoping I'll dish up the inside story on the family scandal.'

'You're selling yourself short.'

He pointed up at the sky and she glanced up to see the first stars starting to emerge. Rolling her shoulders, she unfolded her arms, tried to relax. Reclaiming her hand, he squeezed it and everything inside her tensed again.

'Your insights on taking over the reins of a large enterprise like Garrison Downs—the challenges, the pitfalls…the joys—that's what people want to hear about.'

Nuh uh, he was wrong.

Except…

She frowned. What he described was exactly what she'd wished she'd had a chance to hear and learn from.

'Your experience, that's what's of real use to people on the land. It's gold, Rose. Rose gold.'

And then he grinned as if delighted with the pun and she had to choke back a laugh.

'You have an opportunity to help, to make a real difference. That's why you were invited to be the speaker.'

She had no idea what to say, her mind whirling with the new spin he'd put on the issue.

'Mind you—' he winked '—if you wanted to include some salacious gossip, the tabloids would love you.'

Huffing out a laugh, she tried to run him into a grevillea. 'Very helpful, Lincoln, thank you.'

He grinned, glancing around. 'Your father had the gardens built for your mother, didn't he?'

She welcomed the change of topic. 'Theirs was a whirlwind romance, but once my mother found herself out here so far from family and friends and all that she knew, it was tough for her. She became homesick.'

Her mother's lovely face rose in her mind, the faraway look in her eyes whenever she spoke of her home, and a familiar ache gripped her chest. She did what she could to breathe through it. 'So Holt created this garden for her. It was her pride and joy.' Her solace and her comfort. 'When Da— Holt had New House built, one of the things that excited her most was enlarging the garden. The garden connects both homesteads while providing both households with privacy.'

Rounding the corner of the house she gestured across the lawn to the lights twinkling behind a hedge of lilly pilly—Old House, the original homestead. It must've been a nightmare for Rosamund to move to Garrison Downs and then be forced to live with her mother-in law. Other than their love for Holt, the two women had had nothing in common.

'Did you tell Eve about Cordelia's diary?'

'I told all the girls. Eve's been scouring the place, but so far no luck.'

He squeezed her hand. 'I'd love it if we found it.'

She made herself smile, but things inside her tensed. What did Lincoln expect to find in that diary? Evidence that Garrison Downs still belonged to his family?

She shook herself. 'Tilly would go mad for it.'

He glanced down. In the gathering darkness it was hard to read his expression. 'What's your favourite part of the garden?'

'My mother's was the rose garden. Come and see. We're very proud of it.'

He pulled her to a halt. His thumb brushed the inside of her wrist, back and forth, making her pulse jump and pulling her skin tight.

'I didn't ask to see your mother's favourite part of the garden, I asked to see yours.'

Hers? 'It's not particularly picturesque.' Not in the same way the rose garden was.

'Show me anyway.'

And still that thumb brushed across the sensitive skin of her wrist. Gritting her teeth, she turned them to the right. She *could* ignore it. She *would* ignore it.

Except she couldn't. And the awareness built inside her until she wanted to scream. For heaven's sake, all he was doing was idly running his thumb back and forth. He probably didn't even realise he was doing it!

On the pretence of gesturing to a large gum, she tugged her hand from his again and moved across to sit on the swing that hung from one of its branches—a swing with a seat broad enough for three sisters. 'This is my favourite spot in the garden. Evie, Tilly and I turned this into our unofficial clubhouse.'

And Ana should've been here with them. She started to seethe. If Holt had—

'What did you do here?'

She pulled her mind back. 'Evie would spin tales of princes and princesses and fairy-tale castles while Tilly would regale us with stories of the Taj Mahal and the Colosseum and Stonehenge.'

He gestured. 'May I?'

She shuffled over and he took a seat beside her. Their shoulders touched and she inhaled his scent—clean and fresh, but laced with something darker that had an edge to it, like leather or fresh firewood. It complemented the night perfectly.

'And what about you?'

'It's where I plotted how to make sure I could join the muster when I was thirteen. How to talk my mother into letting me do my last few years of school via correspondence rather than at boarding school. It's where we plotted to sweet-talk our old housekeeper, Mrs Bishop, into making ANZAC biscuits, how to break the news of some misdemeanour to our parents, and how to wrangle someone to take us into Marni.'

His laugh, low and rich, had an added potency in the gathering dark and goosebumps raced across her skin. The moon had started to rise, a large golden disc. She pointed, turning to see if Lincoln had followed the line of her arm, to find him staring at her, his eyes deep and dark.

'Has the swing witnessed any stolen kisses?'

Flirting came as easily to him as breathing. 'I'm sure it's seen its fair share.'

'Any of them yours?'

Maybe it was the beauty of the night—the stars and the scent of roses drifting across the lawn—but she felt suddenly lighter and freer. Since she'd married Lincoln, a weight had lifted from her shoulders. And it made her feel…hopeful. Rather than close him down, she raised an eyebrow. 'Why? Tempted to steal a kiss?'

'More than life itself.'

His eyes blazed in the light of the moon and that dark hungry gaze drifted to her lips. A pulse started up deep inside. He stared at her with the same intensity that he had seven years ago, and she knew in that moment he was going to kiss her.

More to the point, she knew she was going to let him. She wanted to know if her memory of that long ago kiss was real. Or if she'd blown it out of proportion.

Lincoln's mouth lowered towards hers with un-hurried deliberation, and they hovered there between breaths, savouring the moment. Down by the river a spotted nightjar called a series of ris-ing notes.

And then Lincoln's lips were on hers and they were neither urgent nor fierce and yet everything inside her quickened and shifted. Her mouth opened—on a gasp or whether to draw more of him in, she had no idea. But he accepted the invitation without hesitation, one hand cupping the back of her head while he thoroughly plundered and explored. Her fingers curled into the material of his shirt to pull him even closer so she could plunder him back.

Need coursed through her like a grass fire—an instant and fierce conflagration that was mindless and demanding. They careened across the grass, and she couldn't even remember standing. At the last moment, Lincoln turned them, his back crashing into the huge gum behind, his hands gripping her hips as though he'd never let her go. Hell, he'd have bruises. He'd—

But then his mouth was on hers again and there was nothing lazy or slow about it and her mind splintered. Hands slid beneath her shirt—strong and warm against her fevered flesh. Excellent idea. She slid her hands beneath his shirt too, explored the hard contours of his stomach. Slid them upwards to explore that glorious chest, ran the flat of her palms over flat male nipples that beaded intriguingly and made her hungry to explore more.

'Rose.'

Her name sounded ragged, as if dragged from some deep place inside him.

'Rose.'

This time it was accompanied with the tiniest of shakes. She forced her gaze upwards. Eyes slumberous with desire stared down at her and she almost stood on tiptoe to kiss him again. But hands at her ribcage held her in place, and she belatedly realised the question he was asking—did she want this to continue?

Hell, yes.

She swallowed. But…

She swore.

He released her immediately.

She took a couple of steps back, sucking in a breath. She was a virgin. At twenty-nine. And, yes, she knew it was laughable, but there were reasons. If they were to continue, she'd have to tell him.

And she wasn't sure…

She lifted her chin. Why shouldn't she embrace what he had to offer? Surely she was finally due something just for herself? She'd put that side of her life on hold for so long…

His eyes glittered in the dark and a hard thirst gripped her. She wanted him with an intensity that took her off guard, but it didn't automatically follow that she should fight it.

'Do you think we can be lovers without damaging a potential friendship?' she asked, clenching and unclenching her hands.

He nodded and moved a step closer. 'Do you want to become lovers, Rose?'

'Yes.' She held up a hand when he took another step towards her. 'But there's something you ought to know first.'

'Okay.'

She hitched her head in the direction of the homestead. 'C'mon, we need a drink for this.'

They kicked off their shoes, washed their hands, and she led him through to the piano bar—the most grown-up room in the house with its ebony baby grand, glittering chandelier and indulgent white carpet. And Holt's best whisky. Lincoln whistled when she pulled the bottle from behind the bar. She poured them both a generous measure and pushed a glass towards him.

Too keyed up to move to one of the chairs, she paced across to the piano, her feet sinking into the white carpet that was so insanely difficult to keep clean. As kids, they'd never entered this room without permission.

She turned, leaned against the baby grand. 'What I'm about to tell you isn't particularly edifying, but…here goes.' She took a fortifying sip. 'Have you ever made a really bad promise?'

He rested back on a bar stool. 'I suppose we all have.'

'When I was fifteen, my grandmother made

noises about putting Pop in a nursing home.' Her grandfather, Cec Waverly, had been gored and tossed by a mickey bull when he was thirty-eight. It had left him partially crippled.

'Was your granddad that…?'

'Incapacitated? Unwell?' She shook her head. 'My grandmother was simply a mean-spirited woman who wanted to manipulate everyone around her. I begged her not to put Pop in a home, told her he belonged at Garrison Downs.'

The memory could still make her stomach churn. She knew now Holt would never have allowed that to happen, but she'd only been fifteen and so easily manipulated. 'I loved Pop. We were close. He taught me to identify the tracks of wild animals, taught me survival skills necessary to the land, and he taught me how to play chess.'

'Rose, what did you promise?'

She slugged back the rest of her whisky in one hit, let it warm the cold places inside her. 'In return for not putting Pop in a nursing home, I promised my grandmother I'd remain a virgin until my wedding night.'

His head rocked back. She wanted to curl into a ball and hide from his shock.

Don't be a drama queen.

'Why would she demand such a thing?'

'She seemed to think I could use it as some kind of bargaining chip to snare myself *"an important husband"*.' She rolled her eyes. 'Nobody could accuse my grandmother of progressive attitudes.'

Anger burned bright in his eyes. 'Did she demand the same of your sisters?'

'No, thank God. She said I'd be the one to take over the station, that Evelyn and Matilda would leave for what they thought were brighter pastures, which apparently made them fools.' Her hand clenched around her now empty glass. 'She said that as I would be the Waverly to take over Garrison Downs, we couldn't have me doing anything that would bring shame on the family. Quote, *"I won't have you marry someone unsuitable just because you have a bun in the oven."'*

He swore.

'My sentiments exactly.' She attempted a smile. 'In case you don't know, that's a line from the movie *Mamma Mia.'*

He didn't smile back. His hand clenched so hard he'd started to shake. 'Rose, are you telling me you're still a virgin?'

'Yes.' Her cheeks burned, but she refused to look away. 'Not because of that promise. I figured Grandma's lies and manipulations made it null and void. But I didn't figure that out until my first year of university.'

She stared into her glass, wished she hadn't guzzled her drink so fast. 'A few weeks after I started seeing someone though, and before things had progressed that far, my grandmother died.

I came home—for the funeral and to help out where I could—and by the time I returned to university the guy I'd been seeing had moved on to someone else.'

He dragged a hand down his face. 'Rose…'

'Oh, he didn't break my heart, though he sure as hell hurt my pride. But the thing is, no one else has seriously tempted me since.' She swallowed. 'Other than the night of the Bachelor & Spinster ball when I was twenty-two…'

'When we kissed.'

He remembered it too. Something inside her shook, though in relief or fear she couldn't tell. She forced a shrug. 'It seemed stupid to sleep with someone just for the sake of it. It didn't help that I was working my butt off. I completed the face-to-face components of a four-year degree in two. That didn't leave much room for socialising.'

'And since university?'

She eased down to the piano stool. 'There has always been something more important that needed doing, that took precedence. Pop died when I was nineteen, Mum when I was twenty-two. Holt needed me.'

She rubbed a hand over her face. 'I had a rule not to sleep with anyone who worked here, figured that'd be asking for trouble. And it's not a simple hop, skip and jump into town.'

'Rose, it's only an hour to Marni from here.'

It sounded appalling, laid out so starkly. 'I

thought that one day I'd see someone and *bam*—sparks would fly.' She stood and moved across to him. 'And now it has. With you.'

Lincoln stared down at her with eyes that throbbed. And then he stepped back. 'Excuse me, Rose. I need some air.'

Rose stared after him, started at the sound of the front door closing. Moving across to the bar on legs that felt like lead, she poured herself another whisky. But she couldn't drink it. Her stomach churned too much for that.

What did you think was going to happen?

Lincoln was a man of the world with sophisticated tastes, and she'd just proven she was as unsophisticated as they came. Her insides shrivelled to the size of a hard dry nut. He clearly didn't want to mess with a naïve little virgin.

Pressing her palms to her eyes didn't ease the way they burned. Was Lincoln worried the naïve little virgin would fall in love with him? She dragged her hands away. She might not be worldly, but she wasn't an idiot. They both knew this arrangement was temporary.

But Lincoln walking away confirmed what she'd suspected and had been stupid not to heed—that he simply wasn't that into her. She should've listened! If she had she wouldn't be feeling such a fool now.

Instinct continued to tell her that Lincoln wasn't like his father, and she still mostly believed that.

But Clay *was* his father, and she'd be a fool to ignore that fact. And she was through being a fool.

Lincoln wanted Camels Bridge. And he might also be happy to turn a blind eye to any mischief his father caused. Her stomach churned. His kisses might even be a ruse to string her along, lull her into a false sense of security. Discovering she was a virgin, though, might've pricked his conscience. Maybe messing with a virgin was a step too far in whatever skewed code of conduct he operated under.

She abandoned her drink. She needed to get *relations* between her and Lincoln back on a strictly business footing. She refused to let him leave her feeling so exposed and foolish again.

CHAPTER SIX

LINCOLN PACED THE perimeter of the garden, Rose's words echoing in his head. She was a virgin. He'd been about to fall on her like a starving dog. But...

She was a virgin!

He'd had to walk away before he'd done something he'd regret. Like surrendering to his intoxicating greed and taking what she offered with an unholy intensity. Without giving her a chance to catch her breath or think better of her decision. Or before he could work out if he could keep the promise he'd made her—*Do you think we can be lovers without damaging a potential friendship?*

To be Rose's first lover... He'd be a fool to think it wouldn't be momentous. For both of them—him as much as her.

He braced his hands on his knees. She didn't need some impatient, uncontrolled brute pawing at her. She deserved a man who'd take things slow, who'd bring her passion to deliberate but unhurried life, who'd encourage her to explore it without restraint.

He *wanted* to be the man to do that.

In the piano room, all he'd been able to think about was dragging her into his arms and making her his. *Right then.* Kissing her until she was mindless and begging, joining their bodies with a savage joy. His body had shaken with the effort of holding back.

Hence the need for a breather.

Gulping air, he straightened. She needed someone who'd focus just on her and her needs, not themselves. And he *could* be that man.

A wild uninhibited joy flooded him, making him feel more alive than he had in all of his thirty-two years. As he glanced towards the house, the light in Rose's bedroom came on like a beacon—and he answered the call, immediately starting towards it.

Rose opened the French doors on his second tap. She hadn't started getting ready for bed yet, still wore the same jeans and T-shirt she'd had on earlier. It was all he could do not to sweep her up in his arms and kiss her.

'Lincoln, I've had a rethink. And the sex thing?' She shook her head, her voice cold. 'Not going to happen.'

The ground beneath his feet tilted and he battled a sudden wave of nausea. 'You want to tell me why?'

She folded her arms and sent him a wide fake smile—one that appeared deliberately designed to annoy, which incongruously had him battling a grin. She was magnificent.

'I'd be delighted to. I just told you something I've never shared with anyone, and your response was to walk away.'

Hold on. He'd done that so—

'It makes me think you're no more trustworthy than your father. Or my grandmother.'

His head rocked back. He hadn't considered how she might interpret his leaving as he had. His chest clenched tight. His hands opened and closed, feeling strangely bereft. The last thing he'd meant to do was hurt her. 'I'm sorry if my leaving like I did made you feel bad. It was the last thing I meant to do.'

Her only answer was a shrug.

He moistened his lips. 'You want to know why I left like I did?'

'It doesn't really matter now.' She started to close the door. 'It's been a long day. I'm going to bed. *Alone.*'

'I left before I could do something appalling like fall on you like some starving wild animal.'

She froze just for a millisecond, but it was long enough for a sudden gust of breeze to snatch the door from her fingers and send it crashing back into the room. He glanced behind her, his gaze landing on an object sitting on her dresser, and he froze. She followed his gaze and swallowed.

Striding into the room, he seized the piece of

amber sitting there. This was the token he'd given her when he was eleven years old—after she'd witnessed Clay hit him in the general store. Back then, this piece of amber had been one of his most prized possessions.

He turned to her with it on his palm. 'You kept it.'

Reaching out, she took it from him, colour staining her cheeks. 'It always felt like a symbol of a friendship that should've been. But I think I've always been a sentimental idiot where you're concerned.' Her gaze clashed with his. 'I felt bad that you had to put up with Clay and his terrible temper, and over the years I've let that colour my judgement.'

'We promised each other honesty, so I'll give you honesty, Rose. I went on my dating spree seven years ago because you wouldn't go out with me.'

Her eyes widened and her jaw sagged. He felt like an idiot saying it out loud, but in leaving so abruptly, he'd made her feel small and diminished. He'd do anything he could to make up for that.

'Our kiss at the dam that night rocked my world. I wanted more of it. When you wouldn't go out with me, I figured there'd be other women who could make me feel the same way.' He planted his feet, his glare defiant. 'But I was wrong.'

She glanced away, retied her ponytail.

'So the fact of the matter, Rose, is that I can

totally see why you were waiting for another moment like that before sleeping with someone.'

She folded her arms tight across her chest.

'I went looking and didn't find what I was looking for. You stayed put and didn't find what you were looking for. And here we are. Again. Feels like we've come full circle.'

Her eyes throbbed in the dim light of her bedroom lamp.

He advanced on her. 'A woman like you deserves more than to have some guy fall on her and paw at her like an animal. You deserve to be wooed, you should be spoiled, and made to feel beautiful...special.'

Her chin lifted. 'It's a pretty line, but my understanding is that you've had a lot of practice at spinning pretty fictions.'

He bent at the waist until they were eye to eye. 'You shouldn't believe everything you hear.'

She shook her head. 'We're not going to do this.'

His heart dropped to his feet.

'It's too risky. What about tomorrow...and the day after that?' She stabbed a finger at him. 'What I want is for us to develop a halfway decent working relationship and that doesn't include sleeping together. We both know that could complicate things. And complicated is the last thing I need right now.'

He'd missed his chance, had played this all

wrong. And now he needed to back off and give her space.

'What's at stake here for you, Lincoln? A piece of land. For me it's my home and my sisters' home. My livelihood.' She slapped a hand against her chest. 'My *life*.'

She shouldn't define her life based on the station. No matter how profitable that land might be, she was worth so much more than that. An ache spread through his chest. Somewhere nearby a tawny frogmouth's hoot vibrated on the night air.

Rose was carrying the weight of the world on those slim shoulders. He wanted to make her life easier, not harder. It took a supreme effort, but he forced his legs to carry him through the French doors until he stood on the veranda again. 'There's more at stake for me than you give me credit for.'

Her gaze travelled over his face, but she remained silent.

'What happened between Cordelia and Louisa May all those years ago has rippled down through the generations. What happens between us now, Rose, can have the same effect on the generations to come. I don't want to leave a legacy of bitterness and hate in my wake. And I don't believe you do either. I'll do whatever I can to make sure that doesn't happen. You have my word.'

Turning, he disappeared into the darkness before his resolution crumbled, but in that moment he made a resolution. He was going to make this woman fall in love with him or die trying. He was now playing for longer than three months. He was playing for keeps.

Lincoln stared at the contract he held. The kiss in the garden two day's ago had solidified exactly what he was doing here at Garrison Downs; why he'd married Rose; what he was hoping for.

While he wanted to be in a position to prevent his father from causing harm—to both Garrison Downs and himself—and while it was also true that he'd do what he could to mend fences between the two families, what he most wanted was to win Rose's heart.

He'd never found the same fire with any woman that he'd experienced with Rose. He'd gone looking for it, but no woman had inflamed and captivated him the way she had.

And he suspected now they never would.

There'd been a connection between the two of them since that day in the general store. Cemented by their one stolen kiss. At the B & S ball where separately, and unbeknownst to one another, they'd slipped out to catch their breath, take a rest from the noise and revelry. He'd seen her ambling on the opposite side of the dam from him, and at the same time they'd both seen the distressed calf that had been caught in the mud.

Neither of them had hesitated—even though

he'd been wearing a tuxedo and she a fancy ball-gown. They'd waded in and had managed to wrestle the calf free. Her dress had been ruined, her arms and legs caked in mud, splatters on her face and hair, but her eyes had sparkled and she'd laughed.

Taking her hand, he'd helped her back to drier ground where they'd grinned at each other like idiots and then… It felt like a dream when he thought about it now. The grins had faded and something electric had arced between them and his head had dipped towards hers and hers had lifted towards his and their kiss had flared in the night like some bright promise—full of fire and vitality.

They'd eventually stumbled apart. She'd lifted a hand as if to touch her lips, and he'd had wit enough to reach out and stop her, her hands still as muddy as his. But she'd threaded her fingers through his and had squeezed tight. And he'd squeezed back. Then laughter from the nearby group approaching had had them springing apart. One of her sisters had appeared with a few other friends and laughed when she'd seen the state of Rose and her dress. 'Mum's going to pitch a fit when she sees you.'

'Calf in trouble. Dad'll get it.'

'Come on, let's go get you cleaned up.'

And then she'd been moving away from him, but before she'd disappeared she'd turned back—

had sent him a single glance that had burned itself onto his soul.

But she'd refused to go out with him when he'd rung, and he'd never really understood why. After yesterday's kiss, though, he wished he'd stuck around and found out, fought harder to convince her they belonged together.

He stared down at the document he held. After the stunt his father had pulled, she had to be wondering if she'd made a major mistake in marrying him. But maybe this would help.

He had three months to win her trust, to make himself indispensable…to make her fall in love with him. He'd use whatever tools he had at his disposal.

Striding into the living room, he found her curled up on her lounge with some report or other. Rose, he'd discovered, was always working. If she wasn't careful, she'd burn out.

She wore shorts, and the sight of those long legs with their smooth tanned skin had him prickling and itching all over. He ran a finger around his collar only to realise he wasn't wearing one.

'I have something for you.'

With the tiniest of frowns, she took the document he held out to her. With hands in pockets, he watched the emotions play across her face as she read it. Slamming upright, though still reading, she crackled with an outraged energy that had him thinking of summer storms and the way they could light up the entire sky.

That was what Rose was—a natural phenomenon. She might act all cool and reserved and aloof, but underneath this woman was fire and flame, thunder and lightning.

She slapped a hand to the contract. 'You can't do this!'

He grinned, doing his best not to stare at those amazing legs. 'Yeah, I can.'

'You can't just *give* me your plane, your horse, and your cat.'

Holding her gaze, he nodded. 'They're the three things I love most in the world.' Then he aimed for levity. 'Despite appearances to the contrary, I love my father too, but you can't give people away. There are laws against it. I checked.'

She huffed out a laugh. 'Lincoln, be serious. This—'

'I've never been more serious. I want you to trust me. I want you to know that I plan on keeping every promise I've made to you. I want you to believe me when I tell you I'm not working with my father to harm Garrison Downs or your position here in any way.'

She stared at him, her eyes wide and uncertain, but she wanted to believe him, he could see that too.

'If I don't, you get to keep Judy, that's what I call the Cessna, along with Thunder my horse and

Colin. And I know *you* know how much those things mean to me.' Out here, a man's horse was everything. The Cessna was a symbol of freedom, of autonomy. And while Colin wasn't worth anything materially, he'd stolen Linc's heart. Losing any of them would gut him.

She pressed a hand to her brow as if trying to understand why he was doing this—why he'd risk these things.

'Once I've kept all of my promises, I ask that you return that contract to me so I can destroy it.'

She shook the paper at him. 'You've not stipulated that here.'

'I know. I also know if you promise to do it, you will. I don't need that in black and white.'

'You should protect—'

He pressed a finger to her lips. 'I know you're a person of honour. When you make a promise, you keep it. I trust you.'

Straightening, she held his gaze. 'In three months' time, once you've fulfilled all the terms of our agreement, I promise to return this contract to you.'

'Thank you.' Job done. He'd made a start.

And now to induce her to a bit of downtime. He gestured at the television. 'Now, come on, you have me intrigued. Put on an episode of *The Bold and the Beautiful*.' He knew she recorded them. 'I did some research while I was out at Ned's Gorge and there's a villainess who intrigues me.'

'Oh, she's deliciously awful. I love her.'

Curling up on the sofa, she tossed the report to the coffee table. River leapt up beside her, his head on her lap. Lincoln sat on her other side, not too close, feet on the ottoman. Colin leapt up and started to clean himself on Lincoln's lap. She glanced at Lincoln, a quizzical light in her eyes. 'You sure about this?'

'Positive.'

Huffing out a laugh, she reached for the remote.

'All I'm saying is that I don't understand why she had to throw such a big temper tantrum.'

At his side, Rose laughed and the morning air grew brighter as they moved towards a complex of well-maintained outbuildings. Even the red dust seemed tinged with gold. 'It's because she's the ultimate drama queen—*drama* being the operative word.'

'The guy was such a patsy. He let her walk all over him and then he needled her—*deliberately*.'

'It's because he thinks she's in love with his dead brother.'

He halted. 'Isn't she?'

'Nope.' She halted too. 'She was only pretending because he was blackmailing her.'

'You *cannot* be serious.'

'A soap's joy is in all of its crazy sauce over-the-topness, its melodrama.' Her eyes danced.

'But underneath all of that there are some universal truths.'

'Like?'

She swung away, still grinning. 'Perhaps we can explore that more fully with another episode tonight.'

That had him laughing. Maybe soaps would never become his thing, but he'd sure as hell enjoyed sitting beside Rose as they'd watched not one but two episodes last night. 'Nice try, but tonight I'm challenging you to another game of chess.'

'Fine. Now do you want to see the stud or not?'

She'd offered him a tour after breakfast and he'd leapt at the chance. She knew from their pre-wedding phone conversations that he'd eventually like to establish his own stud. 'Yes, please, ma'am.'

With a snort, she pushed into a huge, well-ventilated shed. Inside a central cement corridor was lined on both sides with stalls, many of them with access to yards outside. The Downs' stud stock.

Garrison Downs had one of the most successful breeding programmes in the country. She walked him through their operation, showed him the bulls she hoped would eventually prove as successful as Carnelian Boy, and he couldn't help but be impressed. 'You're doing great things here.'

'Holt had the initial vision. And he made sure to hire the best people.'

'Maybe, but you've the knowledge and the passion to take it to new heights.'

'We'll see.' Her lips twisted. 'The Arteta contract Aaron mentioned yesterday is an exchange programme I've been wanting to set up between us and a Spanish stud who are doing interesting things.'

His ears pricked. 'You brokered the deal yourself?'

She nodded. 'Holt saw the potential when I told him about it, but he wasn't convinced.'

But he could see that she was.

She dragged both hands through her hair, retied her ponytail. 'It's been years in the making… so much red tape, going back and forth so many times… I thought it was all finally in the bag.'

A cold finger raked his spine. 'Any idea what's up?'

'Nope, but as I have a call with Mr Arteta in an hour, I guess I'll find out soon enough.'

He opened his mouth, but she shook her head. 'I now want to introduce you to our pride and joy. Junior here is the latest and will be one of the last of Carnelian Boy's offspring. He's only two weeks old. What do you think?'

He cast an expert eye over the calf and the air whistled between his teeth. 'I think I can honestly say I've never seen a better proportioned bull calf in my life, Rose. He's extraordinary.'

Her swift smile was his reward. 'I'm glad you like him as he's your wedding present.'

CHAPTER SEVEN

SURPRISE AND DELIGHT raced across Lincoln's face. He stared from Rose to the calf and back again. 'I wasn't serious when I asked for Carnelian Boy. I was…'

'Seeing what else you could negotiate? It was business. I don't blame you for that.'

'Want the truth?'

The low chuckle that emerged from the depths of him brushed across the bare skin of her arms, making her want. She hadn't stopped wanting since their kiss in the garden two days ago. She dragged her gaze from that far-too-tempting body. 'Regardless of how unpalatable it might be, I will always choose the truth, Lincoln.' Even if she didn't like it, the truth was something she could work with.

'Your proposal had knocked me for six. I was playing for time while I tried to find my feet again.'

She couldn't think of a single thing to say. She could think of a lot of things she'd like to do.

For pity's sake, stop thinking about kissing him!

He gestured at the stall. 'This is a tremendous gift. You might want to rethink—'

'Or I might not.'

'You—' He broke off, then, 'Your father would strongly advise you against it.'

'Oops.' She hoped her shrug carried every bit of nonchalance she wished she could feel.

His eyes narrowed.

She narrowed hers too. 'And your father is doing cartwheels and singing show tunes at the fact you've given me your cat, your horse, and your plane?'

Those hypnotic lips did that slow-grin thing and she had to look away, pull in a breath. 'You want us to trust each other. You want us to like each other.'

'Rose, I already like and trust you. But, yes, I want that.'

'And I'm choosing to believe you're sincere.'

Please God, don't let her be wrong about this man.

She recalled the haunted expression in his eyes when they'd stood on the south-eastern boundary with evidence of Clay's troublemaking surrounding them. Instinct told her Lincoln wasn't involved, and after his gesture last night...

She'd chosen to believe he wasn't. 'We have a business deal, and I intend to keep my side of the bargain.'

'As do I.'

Please God, let him mean that.

'But this gift…' she nodded at the calf '…isn't about business.'

Dark eyes turned almost black. He took a step closer, and she could hardly breathe. 'What is it about?'

'It's a thank you.'

'For agreeing to your proposal?'

Her mouth went dry. She shook her head. 'For making it as easy as you could. For being kind about everything rather than cocky and arrogant.'

'Cocky isn't my style.' He frowned. 'Rose, I want us to be true partners.'

The way he said *'true partners'* made her chest lurch. The expression in his eyes when his gaze had landed on the piece of amber in her room… the tone of his voice when he'd said he didn't want to leave behind a legacy of hate. The passion in his eyes seven years ago after they'd kissed. The joy and excitement that had raged in her heart…

Blossom nudged Rose's knee, whined. Reaching down, she scratched her ears, tried to get her racing pulse back under control.

If Lincoln broke his promises to her…

Ice crawled across her scalp. It'd break something inside her. Somewhere along the line, she'd become invested in…

What? This marriage?

Not the marriage. *That* was business. But in becoming friends with Lincoln, in forging a connection with him. In working with Kalku Hills rather than against them. If he was toying with her—

Sidestepping him, she leaned her arms against the stall door, stared at the calf. She'd decided to believe him sincere. Worrying and doubting now would only undermine that. If her judgement let her down, if he didn't keep his word, it would hurt her in ways she couldn't begin to imagine. But some things were worth taking a risk for, worth making a fool of yourself over.

She gestured to the calf. 'I know you'd like to start your own stud. This is a gesture of goodwill—a token of my hopes for the brighter future I'm hoping we can forge. But it comes with no strings.'

Reaching down, Lincoln took her hand and lifted it to his lips, brushed a kiss across her knuckles that had her skin tingling. 'I've never been given a finer gift in my life. I will cherish him. And I promise to look after him to the very best of my ability.'

The sheen in his eyes had a lump lodging in her throat. Swallowing hard, she reclaimed her hand. 'I know you will.' After clearing her throat a couple of times, she glanced at her watch. 'I need to get back for my phone call. In the meantime, you need to come up with a name for this guy.'

'I'm going to call him Waverly Rose.'

He said it without hesitation and another lump stretched her throat into a painful ache.

'If that's okay with you?'

She nodded. It was very okay.

'He's going to be the finest stud bull in the country.'

The lump dissolved and she gave a slow grin that ended in a laugh. Lincoln stared, his gaze fixing on her mouth. It had butterflies gathering in her belly. 'He'll be in the top three. Garrison Downs will have the other two.'

He really needed to stop looking at her like that! 'Did you want to chat to Lori, who's in charge of the breeding programme?' She called Lori over and introduced them.

He shook the other woman's hand. 'I'd love to talk to you about what you're doing here, but I'm expecting a delivery that I need to be on hand for.'

Rose nodded when Lori glanced at her. 'When he has the time, it would be great if you could talk him through whatever he'd like to know.'

'Sure thing, Boss. Whenever you're free, Linc, you know where to find me.'

He nodded his thanks and then kept easy pace beside Rose as they made their way back to the homestead.

'You know Jackson?'

She glanced up. 'One of your stockmen, right?'

'One of Kalku's stockmen,' he corrected. 'He's

bringing Thunder over for me this morning, driving my car.'

With a horse float, he'd have had to go the long way around, which would take at least six hours. 'I'd have organised a car and horse for you while you were here.' She kicked herself for not mentioning that earlier.

'I wanted my own. And, anyway, Rose, he's yours now.'

'Only if you break your word.' And she couldn't believe he'd risk his horse, his cat and the Cessna. She'd never put Opal and Blossom up as collateral, not in a million years.

'Anyway, people would talk if Thunder remained at Kalku.'

Frowning, she halted beneath a huge red gum that stood at the edge of the garden. The shadows of the leaves moving in the breeze made intriguing patterns on his face. 'Is there anything else we should do to make this marriage appear real to the wider world?'

One broad shoulder lifted. 'At some stage we should probably go into Marni and shout a round at the Royal to celebrate.'

They should.

'But not today.' He urged her forward again. 'Once Jackson gets here, the two of us will unload and then I'm flying him back to Kalku.'

'We'll give him lunch first. And tell him to

jump in the pool if he wants to cool off. It's a dusty drive.'

'Thanks, Rose.' They vaulted up the steps at the rear of the house and toed off their boots in the mudroom. He held the interior door open with his hip before plucking off her hat and placing it on its usual peg and setting his beside it. 'Want to go for a ride later?'

'Sure.' Jasper, her father's horse, needed exercising. Jasper had been grieving since Holt had died. She tried to spare the stallion whatever time she could.

'Coffee?'

She swung to stare. *Really?* 'That sounds great.' She could get used to this.

Twenty minutes later, she had the phone clasped to her ear. Mr Arteta had proven a tough negotiator over the last two years and she respected that, but she'd thought they'd ironed out every kink and crease in their arrangement.

After greetings had been exchanged, she cut straight to the chase. 'Señor Arteta, I thought we had an agreement. You gave me your word.'

'But you did not inform me of all the information.'

Her brows shot up. 'What information are you referring to?'

'It has come to my ears that the ownership of Garrison Downs is now in question.'

Hot blood turned to ice in a heartbeat. 'I beg your pardon?'

'And that due to a condition in your father's will, your cattle station will pass once more into the hands of the Garrison family.'

How had he heard that? Her hand clenched so hard she started to shake.

'Do you deny it?'

To lie would be the death of the deal. And she didn't want to lie, though she cursed the fact that this news had reached his ears.

'Miss Waverly?'

She pulled herself together. 'There was an ancient stipulation in the will that said the station would only pass to the daughters if they were married.'

'My understanding is that *all* daughters must be married, *si*?'

Her lips twisted. He was not only reliably informed, but well informed. Though he was missing one key piece of information. 'Then you'll be pleased to know that I'm now *Mrs* Waverly. All four Waverly daughters *are* married. You can rest assured that Garrison Downs will remain in Waverly hands.'

'I very much hope you are not mistaken, but I refuse to risk so much in a venture that could so easily turn to dust and ashes. If and when Garrison Downs is once again securely in your hands, Mrs Waverly, we will talk again.'

The line went dead and she stared at the handset before slamming it down. 'What the freaking heck?'

Someone cleared their throat in the doorway and she spun around. *Lincoln.* Holding a tray with two mugs of coffee and a plate of date scones. 'How much of that did you hear?'

'Enough.'

He set the tray down and pushed a mug into her hands. 'I suspect you'd prefer something stronger, but it's still a bit early.'

Far too early, and she didn't want her brain fuzzed by alcohol. 'How did he find out about Holt's will?'

Her words shot out like an accusation and Lincoln's head rocked back. 'I didn't tell my father about Holt's will, Rose. I told him nothing about you and me except that we were getting married.'

She reined in her frustration, ground back her suspicions, forced herself to recall her earlier resolution. 'You told me the day I proposed that you'd keep all I said in confidence. I believe you.'

But did she?

Or was she being a fool?

He raked a hand back through his hair, making him look deliciously rumpled like a hero in a sitcom.

'I don't like to ask this...'

She slammed back.

'But can you trust your staff?'

He meant Aaron. 'My sisters and I haven't told anyone about the will except the men we've married.'

He raised an eyebrow. She grimaced. These things had a way of getting about, but they'd been so careful. 'Aaron shouldered a lot in the months after Holt died. I—we were all in shock...' There'd been so much to do.

'Understandable.'

'And he's finding it hard to relinquish control now. Not because I'm a woman.' Aaron wasn't sexist. 'But I'm younger, less experienced, and I have some views that are different from Holt's.' He missed her father almost as much as she did.

He nodded, but those eyes remained watchful.

'So yeah, he's pushing my buttons and we're clashing a bit, but... I trust him.' And she did.

Beyond Lincoln, framed in the glass of the French doors, red dust billowed along the driveway. She nodded towards it. 'Looks like Jackson's here.'

'I better get out there. But, Rose—' dark eyes met hers '—ring Nate. Find out if anyone has requested to see the will.'

Could they do that? 'Okay.'

Rubbing a hand across her chest, she watched him stride away. If she was wrong about him...

If she was wrong, she could bring all of this

crashing down around their ears. Her sisters would be without their home—a place they could turn to if they ever needed refuge. *She'd* be without her home. She couldn't imagine a life for herself apart from the one she had here at Garrison Downs. Didn't want to imagine it.

Lincoln *could* be stringing her along; he could be working with his father. If he'd told Clay about that ancient conditional bequest...

Reaching out, she gripped the back of Holt's chair. Had she handed Garrison Downs to them on a platter?

He gave you Judy, Thunder and Colin.

He might consider them a small price to pay to win the larger prize of Garrison Downs.

Deep inside she didn't want to believe that. Deep inside some instinct urged her to believe he was a man of honour.

'Your judgement has always been sound, Boss.'

She batted her father's words away. She'd been wrong about *him*. But if her judgement let her down now...

She couldn't bear to think about it. She recalled Pop's words from long ago.

'This land is our legacy for all the generation to come, for all the children that are yet to be born.'

If she lost it, she'd never forgive herself.

Pressing her palms to her eyes, she forced herself to think. *Right.* She pulled them away. She'd act as cool and calm as she knew how. But from now on she'd watch and assess Lincoln's every move, weigh everything he said and did. Then she'd decide what to do.

When he dropped Jackson back at Kalku, Lincoln searched for his father, but Clay had gone to ground.

He left a note on Clay's desk, as well as instructions, with both Jackson and the station cook, requesting his father call him. Instinct told him Clay was behind the current mischief Rose was dealing with, but how the hell had he found out about that conditional bequest?

Rose trusted Aaron, but…Aaron had a chip on his shoulder the size of the ridge country to the north.

Once back at the Downs, he toed off his boots in the mudroom, the racket of a vacuum cleaner sounding from inside. Even given the lushness of the lawns surrounding New House and the nightly watering that damped it down, the red dirt still found its way inside.

Silence sounded and Lindy walked through from the formal living room, wiping her hands on a cloth. She smiled when she saw him. 'I have a message for you from Rose.'

He maintained a lazy posture, but things inside him pulled tight. 'Yeah?'

'Drink, Lincoln?'

'I'll help myself to something, Lindy, you don't need to wait on me.' Ambling through to the kitchen, he opened the fridge and pulled out a jug of homemade lemonade, poured himself a glass. 'What did Rose have to say?'

Did his voice soften whenever he said his new wife's name or was that just his imagination?

'That something's come up and she can't go riding with you this afternoon. She was needed elsewhere.'

Needed? Or was that a convenient excuse to avoid him?

Hooking out a chair, he sat, silently cursing his father. He and Rose had made progress in the last couple of days—he still couldn't believe the generosity of her gift this morning. Everything he'd learned about her since they'd married had consolidated what he already knew—Rose was the epitome of generosity and integrity. And beneath that hard-working, cool, calm and collected façade lived a passionate heart.

But a part of her had to now suspect him in league with his father.

Glancing up, he found Lindy watching him. Downing his lemonade in one go, he sent her an easy smile. 'Guess that means I get first shower.'

Lindy twisted a tea towel in her hands. 'Linc, you need to know that for Rose the station comes first.'

Damn it. How glum had he looked?

'She's—'

'It's a big responsibility,' he cut in. 'And it's been hard since her father died.' He didn't want anyone thinking he felt neglected. Jeez, pathetic much? 'Anyway, it wasn't Rose I was thinking of just then, but my father.'

She grimaced. 'Have a run-in with him when you were over at Kalku?'

He didn't answer, just rolled his eyes and said, 'Family,' in his drollest voice, making her chuckle.

But when he stood under the shower a short time later, hot water beating down on him, Lindy's words came back to him.

'For Rose the station comes first.'

A month ago he'd have agreed with her, but now…

Lifting his face to the spray, he rinsed the shampoo from his hair. As much as she loved the place, it wasn't Garrison Downs that came first for Rose. It was her sisters.

He envied the bond she shared with them.

Rose, though, had a big heart. He hoped she'd find room for him in there too—once he'd proven himself to her. Closing his eyes, he let the water beat at him. Any other scenario didn't bear thinking about. Any other scenario would tear the heart from his chest.

Linc glanced up when Rose returned with yet another folder. That was the third time in an hour. He folded his arms and raised an eyebrow.

'What?'

'Why aren't you working in the office? It'd be more efficient than all of this toing and froing.'

She plonked back down on the sofa. She wore shorts again. He tried not to notice. 'It still feels like Holt's office, not mine.'

It had to be hard surrounded by all of those memories. 'Then do something to make it yours.'

'Like what?'

'Change the paintings, go for a new colour scheme, fill it with your own knick-knacks.'

'That'd feel like sacrilege. And anyway—' she waved a hand at the room '—when I'm out here with the TV and chess set I can pretend I'm not really working.'

He raised his eyebrow higher.

'Anyway, you can't talk. You don't seem to be making much progress on whatever it is you're working on.'

'That's true enough.'

She frowned. 'What are you working on?'

'Edits for the latest edition of my book.'

She blinked, leaned towards him. 'Did you just say…you've *written*—'

'*Co*-written.'

'A *book*?'

He rifled through the pile, located the earlier edition and handed it to her.

She stared at the cover, turned to the title page. 'You have a PhD in Economics? You're *Dr* Lincoln Garrison?'

He shrugged.

She stared at him, stared back at the book. 'You've written a book on *economic theory*?'

'*Co*-written with my thesis supervisor.'

'Who just happens to be a professor with thirty years' experience who's considered a leading light in the field.'

She gaped at him. He shrugged again.

'Why don't we know about this? Does your father know?'

'Why should you? And yes.'

'Because you're a local boy! Everyone would be so pleased for you. So proud. And rather than teasing you for—' She broke off with a gulp.

'Being a hard-partying playboy?'

She eased back, folded her arms. 'You haven't been partying hard, though, have you? You've been working on your PhD and writing a book and...?'

She gestured for him to fill in the other gaps. 'Doing the odd guest lecture and some private consulting.'

She stared at him for a long moment. 'Why have you been hiding your light under a bushel?'

'The people who need to know know, Rose. And, besides, I did party hard there for a couple of years.'

Blue eyes sharpened. Slowly she nodded. 'You don't want to make your father look like a complete and utter clown, that's why.'

Her perception shouldn't surprise him.

'You can't win with that man, can you? You go away and do something amazing like this…'

She thought it amazing? His chest expanded.

'Yet rather than brag about your accomplishments, he complains to all and sundry that you've abandoned him and left him to run the place on his own, and…*dismisses* you as shallow and irresponsible. Even though you come back every muster to lend a hand.'

That just about summed it up.

'And, when you are home, he won't listen to your ideas for improvements to the place.' She held up his book. 'When you clearly have the expertise to advise him. Why not?'

Her eyes flashed and he had to fight the urge to reach for her. 'Because he wants to be the one to singlehandedly turn Kalku's fortunes around. He wants the kudos for turning it into as thriving an enterprise as Garrison Downs.' His father refused to relinquish control. He was driven to try and achieve the same level of success that Holt had—to enjoy the same respect and esteem. Lincoln's arguments always fell on deaf ears.

'And that right there is why he's going to fail. Nobody can do it all. A good manager understands their individual team members' strengths and utilises them.' She tossed her reports to the floor. 'I've had enough for one day. Game of chess?'

'Absolutely.'

'You be white this time and we'll see if we get any further through this game than we did the last one.'

'I'll be your white knight whenever you want, Rose.'

'You think these up on the spur of the moment or store them for the right occasion?'

But her lips twitched, and he found himself grinning.

They sat in their usual spots—Rose on the sofa, Linc on the ottoman. River rested his head on Linc's foot, while Colin butted his head against Rose's left arm.

'Give over, you crazy cat.' Pushing him to his back, she scratched under his chin without looking at him. Colin wrapped his front legs around her arm, his purr as loud as a tractor.

Lincoln made his opening move. 'Can I ask you something?'

'Sure.'

'Why wouldn't you date me seven years ago?'

She froze. Easing back, she swallowed. 'I wanted to.'

'But?'

'Do you remember running into me and Mum in Marni the week after the B & S ball?'

He did. He'd done his level best to get Rose alone, but it had proven impossible with Rosamund there.

She moistened her lips. 'Then the following weekend the Marni Cup was on.'

It had been winter. The season of outback social activities. He'd tried to get Rose alone that time too, but hadn't managed it. There'd been too many people, too many distractions. Their eyes had caught and held more than once, though. When he'd smiled at her, she'd smiled back.

'My mother took me aside a few days later, said she'd noticed the way you looked at me.'

He'd wanted to kiss her. He still did.

'And the way I looked back.' She stared at her hands and things inside him clenched. 'She told me there was something I needed to know.'

A vice squeezed his chest. What had Rosamund told her?

'Lincoln, Clay once did his very best to cause trouble in my parents' marriage—insinuating to each of them that the other was being unfaithful.'

His stomach plummeted.

'I was shocked. I said it would never have worked, that their marriage was too strong. She said, *"It is now, but there was a time when it had the potential to cause real mischief. Did cause real mischief."*'

Colin batted his head against her arm. She curled her fingers into his fur as if seeking comfort. Lincoln ached to reach across and draw her onto his lap.

'I now know Mum knew about Holt's affair.

I suspect your dad was just flinging mud in the wild hope it would cause trouble. Which it almost did.'

Acid churned in his gut. 'My father has been an unhappy man most of his life.' The words emerged from numb lips, a fire banking under old hurts.

'My mother said it would hurt them to have Clay in their inner circle.' Her throat bobbed as if she'd swallowed a tennis ball. 'She also said that if it was true love she'd never stand in my way, that love was too precious.' Her gaze lifted. 'But, Lincoln, we barely knew each other.'

He nodded. He didn't blame her, not for a moment.

'And then she died so unexpectedly. And while I knew you weren't like your father, Holt needed me in ways he never had before. I couldn't add to his burdens.'

'I'm sorry, Rose. I'm sorry my father has been the cause of so much pain for your family.'

She reached out and squeezed his hand. 'You're not responsible for your father's actions. None of us ever considered that you were.'

But it didn't change the fact that his surname was Garrison.

She bit her lip. 'Maybe I shouldn't have told you. It paints your father in an ugly light.'

'I'm glad you did.' But things inside him pulled tight.

The phone rang. Reaching across, Rose lifted the receiver. 'Hello?'

Shaking Colin free, she picked up a bishop to move it—

Linc blinked when she placed it back on its original square.

'One moment, please.' Covering the receiver, she grimaced. 'Speak of the devil...it's your father.'

His mouth tightened. 'I left a message for him to call. Thought he'd ignore it.'

They both stood and she handed him the receiver, ducking beneath the cord, clearly intent on giving him some privacy, but he hooked an arm around her waist and pulled her back against him.

'Dad.' With Rose so close, he started to throb.

'What was so darn important I had to ring you asap?'

Linc cut to the chase. 'I want to know who your contact at Garrison Downs is. I want to know who's feeding you information.'

'Don't know what you're talking about.'

He'd always been able to tell when his father was lying. 'I know you're behind the trouble Rose is having with her contracts.'

Clay gave an ugly laugh. 'And what if I am?'

Rose glanced up, her eyes wide.

'Serves both her and Holt right for counting their chickens. Arteta had the right to know the truth.'

Gently detaching his arm, Rose plonked down on the ottoman, fondled River's ears when he padded over to her. Linc missed her warmth, the feel of having her so close.

'And what *is* the truth, Dad?'

'That you're a *traitor*!'

Clay shouted the words so loud Rose winced.

'I've seen the will—'.

Linc sat beside her and held the phone between them so she could listen in.

'How?'

'I have my sources.'

Who here was feeding him information?

'You great big lumbering lug!'

Rose's mouth dropped open. Snapping it shut, she retied her ponytail.

'You've played right into that hussy's hands.'

Linc's hands clenched so hard he started to shake, but Rose nudged him. Mirth brightened her eyes, turning them an intriguing shade of opal. *Hussy?* she mouthed silently, and he found himself grinning then too.

'I'm going to tell you how you're going to fix this. First thing in the morning you're coming home and we're going into Adelaide to have this marriage annulled. And then we're going to start court proceedings and take back what's ours.'

Linc shook his head. His father's bitterness had become an obsession. 'Garrison Downs was never ours, Dad. And despite the name on the front gate—Garrison Downs is Waverly land through and through. It's time you came to terms with that.'

'You listen here—'

'I'm not annulling my marriage to Rose, I'm not divorcing her, or giving you any extra rope with which to hang yourself.'

'For heaven's sake, Linc, you idiot! Think with your head for once rather than a different part of your anatomy. You always had the attention span of a flea, but—'

The phone was snatched from Linc's hand.

'Nobody speaks to my husband like that.' Rose's eyes flashed. 'What a dreadful man you are, Clay. And a terrible father. What gives you the right to speak to anyone like that, let alone your own son?'

'Well, we all know what a sterling father Holt turned out to be, don't we?'

She paled and Linc feared that if his father had been in the room, he'd have punched him.

Her chin lifted. 'Holt had his faults, as we're all well aware, but he never put his daughters down. He never called them awful names or complained about them all over town. He respected us and made sure we knew we were loved. *That's* what a good parent does.'

She blinked as if her words had surprised her.

The line went dead. She stared at it. 'And he never hit us,' she added in a harsh whisper. Slamming the receiver down, she paced around the room, River at her heels as if to give her comfort.

'Doesn't it bug you, the way he talks to you?' Her eyes spat fire.

'I don't let it bother me any more.'

She stabbed a finger at him. 'You shouldn't let anyone speak to you like that.'

She looked magnificent fired up in outrage, and his hunger burned hot and fierce. He pointed at the phone. 'You stuck up for me.'

'I know, I know, you can fight your own battles.'

She started pacing again. River moved to sit in front of Lincoln, stared up at him expectantly. She swung back. 'Except you weren't.'

In two strides he stood in front of her, capturing her hands. 'There's more than one way to win a war, Rose. And I'm winning this one by refusing to allow his bitterness to infect me, by living my life the best way I see fit.'

Hauling in a breath, she nodded. 'You're doing a fine job of it too, Lincoln. You should be proud of yourself…proud of all you've achieved…proud of the man you are.'

Her words punched through him.

Her gaze lowered to his mouth, her pupils dilating.

He had no idea who moved first, but their mouths moved together, hot and hungry, and wildly out of control. Falling down to the ottoman, he took her with him. She kissed him like a starving woman, like a drowning woman, like a woman who wanted everything.

Pulling her flush again him, he let his hands rove across her back, down her hips…lifting her until she half straddled his thighs, both of them balancing precariously on the ottoman. He had to brace one hand behind him to prevent them from toppling over.

She gripped his shoulders, that sweet mouth continued to ravage his and he kissed her back with the same hunger. He slid his hand up the bare skin of her thigh and she dragged her mouth from his to pull air into her lungs. When he pressed the hard ridge in his trousers against the juncture of her thighs, a moan left her lips.

Spots danced across his eyes, but he gathered together the shreds of his control. She'd said she didn't want this, and he wasn't losing her trust now. Claiming one more drugging kiss, he stood and lowered her feet back to the floor, but he didn't release her. 'You said you didn't want this.'

She stared at him, breathing hard, her fingers clinging to his arms as if needing to hold onto something solid.

'Just for the record, I do, but…'

Reaching up, she pressed her fingers to his lips, the pulse in her throat fluttering like a wild thing. 'I do too. And I'm tired of fighting it.'

A surge of heat and need nearly unmanned him. 'Can I tell you what I want?'

She nodded.

'Two nights—you and me alone with no one else around. I know muster is starting, but you'll have me to help when we get back.'

He didn't want Lindy in the house with her vacuum cleaner and dusting cloth. He didn't want Aaron coming in with some disaster. He didn't want Eve coming over for afternoon tea and a gossip. He wanted Rose to be all his for two days. He wanted to show her how good it could be between them.

'I want to do things to you that will make you scream.' He wanted to bliss her out so much she'd never want to let him go.

Her eyes widened. The pulse at her throat pounded like a wild thing. 'In the morning we'll take some supplies and head out to my favourite place on the station.' Her voice was nothing more than a husky whisper.

'Swag rolls and tents?'

'There's a cottage.'

'Sounds perfect.'

She took a step away from him, as if needing air. 'Pack your swimming trunks.'

'We're not going to need clothes, Rose—any clothes.'

'Then pack sunscreen.'

He laughed, but then imagined rubbing sunscreen across her naked flesh. His breath sawed in and out of his lungs. Backing up, he turned and left before the curve of Rose's lips and the way her eyes glittered could unman him.

CHAPTER EIGHT

ROSE PULLED HER four-wheel drive to a halt beside a rustic two-room cabin, her stomach coiled tight, heat throbbing in places she shouldn't be thinking about just yet.

Lincoln raised an eyebrow. 'This is your favourite place on Garrison Downs?'

'I'll show you why in a bit.' She couldn't believe her voice sounded normal. 'C'mon, let's set up.' She'd focus on the practicalities rather than the burning need building inside her, rather than the memory of Lincoln's lips on hers, his hands on her overheated skin and—

Stop it!

Lincoln did a reconnaissance of the cabin while she collected the blow-up air mattress. He grinned when he saw it. 'Nothing but the best for the Lady of the Manor.'

'Just call me Princess Rose.'

'You're not a princess, Rose, you're a queen.'

The tone of his voice—low and husky—and the light in his eyes made her go shivery and weak-kneed.

He'd swept the floor with the old broom and pointed it now at the air mattress. 'I suppose it's my job to pump that up?'

'As much as I'd love to see your muscles gleaming with the effort...'

He nearly dropped the broom. *Ha!* Look at her being sassy.

'This is one of those self-inflating numbers.'

Setting it to the floor, she pulled the appropriate cord and the queen-sized air bed promptly inflated. Lincoln eyes darkened. When they lifted to hers, he moistened his lips as if parched, and an answering thirst raked through her.

Silently they returned to the car for the next load. She was aware of his every step, could imagine the heat from his body and the shape—

Gritting her teeth, she grabbed an armful of bedding and stalked back to the cabin. Rather than her usual swag roll, she'd brought quilts and pillows, and she arranged them over the mattress now.

Standing back, she admired her handiwork.

'A bed fit for a queen,' Lincoln said directly behind her when he eventually brought their bags in and set them on the floor.

Was it too much? 'I wanted to make it look nice.'

She rolled her shoulders. Maybe—

Lincoln turned her, cupped her face in those big strong hands, and her pulse went crazy and so did her breath. Naked need had to be plastered across her face.

'It's perfect. I love it. I want to fix it in my mind so I'll never forget.'

She'd never forget the way he looked at her this very moment. Not if she lived to be a hundred and twenty.

His gaze lowered to her lips and things inside her leapt. He was going to kiss her and—

Releasing her, he took two steps back, and she remembered his words from earlier in the week— *'I won't fall on you like some starving beast.'* Maybe they were both trying to be on their best behaviour. The thought gave her heart.

'I didn't think to bring a camera.' She kept her voice light, shooed him back into the front room, forced herself away from the temptation of that bed. Mobile reception was non-existent out here. She'd left her phone at home. They had the satellite phone in case of an emergency.

'I did.'

She pulled to a halt in the front room. He'd been busy. While she'd been making the bed, he'd unpacked the rest of the car. The Esky keeping their food and drinks cold rested in the corner beside the airtight container of dry food as well as the crockery and cutlery. It weighed a tonne and she'd planned to leave it in the back of the four-wheel drive and yet Lincoln hadn't broken a sweat bringing it inside.

'Say cheese!'

A flash went off, making her blink.

'I thought a few holiday snaps could be fun.'

He sauntered across, bent down until they were eye to eye. 'But no naked photos, okay?'

All she could do was nod. But, of course, all she now wanted was to see him naked. Which was probably his plan, and the thought made her laugh.

'Okay, now is the time to don your swimmers if you want to wear them.' Grabbing the towels she'd slung over a chair, she sauntered outside.

'Are you planning on skinny-dipping, Rose Waverly?'

His voice was filled with laughter and she grinned at the sky. 'I'm wearing my swimmers under my clothes.'

He appeared a few moments later, wearing swimming trunks and a T-shirt. He winked at her and took the towels. 'Thought I'd better be a gentleman.'

She wanted to say, *What a shame*.

He gestured around. 'This seems an odd spot for a stockman's cottage. Especially one of this size.'

A flock of budgerigars lifted from the golden grasses nearby and flew off in a bright flash of green. 'That's because it's not. It's a holiday cottage Holt built for us.' She set off up the track. 'We'd come out here a couple of times a year for some R & R. We loved it.'

They walked steadily upwards for five minutes. Topping the rise, they eased around a sharp bend, and Rose gestured in front of them. 'And now you can see why.'

Red sandstone cliffs rose up all around—grand, ancient, timeless. Beneath them stretched a large rock pool. Still and deep, the water reflected the sky above.

Lincoln let out a low whistle.

'It's something, isn't it?' she murmured.

'I've not heard a whisper about this place before. It's amazing.'

'It's called Cordelia's Leap.'

Named for one of his ancestors.

He turned, and their gazes caught and clung. 'Thank you for bringing me here.'

For no reason at all—or maybe for *all* the reasons—her mouth went dry. She swallowed again, cleared her throat, dragged her gaze away from midnight eyes—eyes that belonged in a bedroom—and shucked off her shorts and T-shirt in double-quick time before remembering she'd meant to make a seductive show of it. Except she needed a cold dousing *now*.

Lincoln's lips parted and his chest rose and fell, his eyes devouring her.

'The water is cold. And deep,' she shot over her shoulder, before vaulting lightly across the rock platform and diving in.

Gah! The water was *freezing*. She welcomed

the shock of it, though—the way it cleared the fog around her brain, the way it chased away the thudding heat that had her in its grip.

Surfacing in the middle of the pool, she turned back to face him. The heat immediately built through her again as he hauled his shirt over his head in one smooth motion, and she was finally free to admire those powerful shoulders and broad chest. He looked as rugged, grand and timeless as the sandstone surrounding them.

And he was hers. It might only be in this moment, or for a few days…or for a few months at most. But the knowledge that this man was married to her and that they were going to become intimate had a thrill humming deep inside—not some temporary frisson either, but a bone-deep vibration. She had no idea what it meant, but she didn't care.

He dropped his shirt beside her clothes. Pausing, he bent down, and when he stood again he held a box in his hand. Turning it over in his fingers, he kinked an eyebrow in her direction.

The box of condoms must've fallen out of her shorts' pocket. 'I'm a safety girl.' It was a line from the movie *Pretty Woman* and she'd always wanted to use it. 'One unexpected pregnancy in the family is quite enough.'

Dropping the box on their pile of clothes, he sauntered down to the water's edge—unhurried, in control, and she'd never wanted a man more.

He didn't hesitate when his feet touched the water, but strode in and was in front of her in four powerful strides of those beautiful arms.

'You are beautiful.' She didn't mean to say the words out loud, but couldn't hold them back.

'So are you.'

No man had ever called her beautiful before, but the expression in his eyes had her believing him—*he* found her beautiful.

One strong arm went around her waist and he pulled her flush against him. Their legs brushed against one another and she flattened her palms against his chest to steady herself.

'I'm not going to ravish you out here in this extraordinary place, Rose.'

'No?'

She couldn't keep the disappointment from her voice and a sudden gleam lit his eyes. 'Those rocks look hard and unforgiving, and when we make love I want you focussed on nothing but me and pleasure. But we can play, if you'd like.'

Both of his hands slid down her sides, his thumbs brushing the sides of her breasts making her gasp. They made a slow sensual journey all the way to her hips. Hooking his hands beneath her thighs, he locked them around his waist, and one fingertip slid beneath the elastic of her swimsuit to travel from her hip, and slowly-oh-so-slowly around.

It stopped. 'I could provide you with some...

temporary relief.' If possible, those eyes darkened further. 'I'd love to make you come apart right now.' That fingertip moved again.

She wanted that too—desperately. But for their first time she wanted him with her. 'Fair's fair, then.' She could barely make her voice work. 'As long as the play is two-sided, and I get to do the same to you.'

Her hands made a bold exploration along his shoulders and across his chest, her fingers tip-toeing down his abdomen—the muscles, that gloriously defined six-pack, all clenching in the most flattering manner—to dip below his waist-band. Before they could reach their destination, she found her hands empty and she was treading water again.

'I'm trying to play the gentleman here and not rush you, but I want you too much.'

He'd moved several feet away, and he breathed heavily, labouring over his words. His face looked ravaged and she finally glimpsed the control he'd imposed on himself.

She gestured between them. 'Mutual,' she whispered.

He moved closer but didn't touch her. 'This water is freezing, but I burn for you. I want you *now*.' The words were raw and filled with need, and something aching and primitive soared free inside her.

Without another word, she swam for shore.

He kept pace beside her. When they reached the rocks, he lifted her out, but released her as soon as her feet hit solid ground. They towelled off, put their shoes on, but didn't bother with the rest of their clothes. Taking his hand, she led him back to the cabin.

He closed the door behind them. Holding his gaze, she lowered the straps of her simple one-piece and peeled the suit from her body to stand before him naked. She didn't want to be coy, and she wanted all barriers between them gone. He drank her in like a starving man. He started towards her, but she held up a hand and gestured. 'Your turn.'

He sent her one of those maddeningly slow grins. 'You'd like to see me naked, Rose?'

The blood pounded in her ears. 'More than life itself.'

He obliged. Flipping open the snap on his trunks, he let them fall to his feet before stepping out of them.

Lincoln was built on the most perfect lines she could imagine for a man. He was big. But perfectly proportioned. And she wanted what was about to happen with every atom of her being.

The appreciation burning in Rose's eyes almost undid him.

Lincoln gathered together the ragged shreds of his control and pulled them tight. He wanted her with a primitive need he'd not experienced before. He wanted her in ways he hadn't known a man could want.

But more than that he wanted to make this special—he would *not* rush. Sauntering across, he snaked a hand beneath her hair and tilted her head, claimed her mouth in an unhurried kiss. Her lips, soft and pliant, opened beneath his, and he tasted her slowly and thoroughly, memorising the shape of her mouth, the texture of her lips, the taste of her. She kissed him back with a hunger she didn't try to hide, with nothing held back. Her arms slid around his neck and her body pressed against his and stars burst behind his eyelids. He had to drag his mouth away to gulp air into starved lungs. 'You're sure about this, Rose?'

'Positive.' She swallowed. 'You?'

Her flash of vulnerability caught at him. 'Never been surer about anything in my life.' Before he'd finished speaking he was pressing kisses against her neck, grazing her earlobe with his teeth. A gasp, a tiny moan, and her body arching into his. Her hands reached out to touch and explore and while he hungered to feel her hands on his burning flesh, he couldn't risk it just yet.

Capturing her wrists lightly in one of his hands, he held them behind her back. 'What are you—?'

Her shocked cry when he closed his mouth around one nipple, the way it beaded as he lathed it with his tongue, dragged a moan from him too.

'Lincoln.' She almost sobbed his name.

'I want to learn your body, Rose.' He kissed his way across to her other breast, his fingers brushing against the side of it, while his lips and tongue applied themselves to pebbling it into urgent hardness.

The way her breath sawed in and out, the way she moved restlessly against him, the gratifying sounds she made—

With a wrench, she pulled her hands free. 'I want to learn your body too. I want to discover what makes you weak at the knees, what makes you tremble. I want—'

Capturing her hands, he pressed a kissed to both palms. 'Sweetheart, my control is thin.' Nearly non-existent. 'If you touch me now, I can't guarantee I'll be able to contain myself. You can explore my body to your heart's content later this afternoon or tonight or tomorrow. I promise.'

Eyes the colour of sapphires glittered in the light pouring in at the window. That colour would stay with him till his dying day.

'For now, please let me focus on you. Please?'

Her eyes grew suspiciously bright. Wordlessly, she nodded. Then she captured his face in her hands. 'I want you with me this first time, Lincoln.'

He'd planned to make her come first with his lips and tongue.

'Please let me have that.'

Nodding, he lifted her into his arms and strode into the bedroom, laid her down on the mattress among the nest of quilts. And then all talking stopped as he applied himself to her pleasure. Kissing her until she panted, working his way down her body until she arched and moaned. Her cry when he touched his mouth to the sensitive heart of her made him feel invincible. He kissed and licked and touched until his name was dragged from her throat. Only then did he sheath himself in a condom and kiss his way back up her body.

Desire-slicked eyes gazed into his. 'I want you, Lincoln. *Now*.'

But he felt the unconscious stiffening of her body, and he had every intention of dispelling it before joining their bodies and making them one. His fingers moved down to damp curls, trailing through them, tugging gently, a finger sliding over her most sensitive nub. Her hips lifted, her legs parted and moved restlessly.

'You taste like the finest wine.' He slid a finger inside her, the silken feel of her almost undoing him. 'I love touching you and feeling you.'

'*Lincoln*.'

His name was a long, low moan and he saw that she was lost again, a slave to the pleasure he was providing, and only then did he nudge himself against her entrance and, meeting no resistance, slide inside.

Her pulsing heat had him clenching his jaw. Her eyes flew open and stared into his. He brushed her hair from her face. 'Did I hurt you?'

She shook her head. 'I thought—'

Her breath caught when he moved and her head fell back. 'Oh, God, Lincoln, you feel so good.'

'That was the plan, sweetheart.'

Short fingernails dug into the muscles of his back. 'I'm sorry,' she panted. 'I have to touch you. I need to hold onto something solid before I…'

He clenched his jaw harder, kept moving rhythmically, steadily. Her body moving with his— urgent, seeking. He'd have to start reciting his times tables soon. 'Before you…?'

Her breath came in short sharp gasps. 'You said you wanted to make me scream.'

'More than life itself,' he gritted out.

'And… I am going to scream!'

With an exultant cry that rang through him like a bell, her muscles clenched all around him as she found her release. The pull and pulse that enclosed him startled a shout from him too—of surprise, pleasure, joy. His body took on a rhythm of its own then, demanding, seeking, wanting everything—all of this woman—as he hurtled into a kaleidoscope of sensation and release.

He came back to himself, to find he'd collapsed on top of her. Probably crushing her. He started to move away, but her hands on his back flattened—

a silent plea for him to remain where he was. Taking some of the weight on his forearms, he stared down at her flushed face—her eyes still closed, damp tendrils of hair curling around her temples—and something in his chest lurched. He forced himself to roll away. They lay side by side, staring up at the ceiling. Reaching out, he took her hand, threading his fingers through hers. 'You okay?'

'I'm more than okay, Lincoln. That was…'

'Yeah.' He couldn't find words for it either. 'It really was.'

'You were worth waiting for.'

He turned his head to meet her gaze. 'So were you.' And he meant it. He'd waited seven long years. And he'd wait another seven if he had to.

There was no going back now and the realisation had an icy hand squeezing his heart. He'd always considered himself half in love with her— she fascinated him, he found her attractive—but he hadn't known her, not really. But he did now in a very real and elemental way. He knew her sense of honour, had witnessed her love for her sisters, saw how hard she worked, and now he'd experienced her passion. He'd made love to this extraordinary woman and it slammed into him now that he never wanted to let her go.

'You're looking awfully serious all of a sudden.'

He crashed back, made himself grin, pointed at his face. 'This is the look of a man who is suddenly ravenous. Is it lunchtime yet?'

'I think we can make our own rules up while we're here. If we want it to be lunchtime, then it's lunchtime.'

Leaping up, she grabbed his T-shirt. 'May I?' At his nod, she hauled it on over her head. It came to mid-thigh, and, while he much preferred naked Rose, it looked cute on her.

She shot him a sassy look over her shoulder. 'I've always wanted to do this. In all the best soaps, after a couple have made love, nine times out of ten she ends up wearing his shirt.'

He couldn't help but laugh.

Planting her hands on her hips, she nodded. 'That's better. Now let's get you fed, and then maybe a bit later...'

That hot gaze roved down his body with naked appreciation and he found himself going hard again.

She stared as if fascinated. Resting his hands behind his head, he did his best to look hot and sexy. 'And a bit later?'

The pulse at the base of her throat fluttered. 'Maybe we can do that again.'

'You know what, Rose? I don't think it is lunchtime just yet.' Reaching out, he tugged her down on top of him.

'So I can have my wicked way with you now?'

'Absolutely.'

With a delighted grin, she set about doing exactly that.

* * *

They ate a late lunch of salad, bread and cheese—cleaning up afterwards and stowing the food safely away, not wanting to encourage the wildlife to explore their sanctuary. Yawning and lazy, they napped. When they woke, he made tea and they sat outside to watch the sky flame with late afternoon colour as the sun descended in the west and the day lost its heat.

'I don't know if this is the right time or not, Lincoln, but can I ask you a personal question or two?'

'I wouldn't mind asking you a couple myself.'

He wouldn't ask her how she felt about spending a lifetime with him. Not yet. It was too soon.

Folding her arms, she stood, her eyes wary. 'You want to ask about Holt and his affair, and how we all really feel about Anastasia.'

He stood too. 'I'd like to know about all of that, sure, but they weren't the questions I had in mind.'

She blinked. 'Oh?'

He refused to be drawn. 'Ladies first.'

'Would you like to come for a walk?' She pointed. 'I'm hoping to find some pretty rocks beneath the ridge along there. Ana, who makes gorgeous things—' she held up her wrist to display her bracelet '—might like them.'

'Sure.'

They walked and fossicked. Tenderness and an

unfamiliar dread warred inside him. He'd always sensed making love with Rose would rock his world, but he hadn't realised how deeply. Hadn't realised it would bind him to her in a way he would never be able to change.

Don't think about that now.

For now, he'd focus on being what she needed him to be. And pray to God that he could win her heart.

'Ask your questions, Rose.'

Eyes bluer than the sky above turned to him. 'You're under no obligation to answer or—'

'Ask your questions, and I'll answer if I can.'

Bending down to pick up a pebble, she turned it over in her fingers. 'Your father treats you terribly, and yet you tell me you love him. What kind of relationship do you have with him?'

He took the pebble from her—a shard of granite—and replaced it with a piece of quartz, a ribbon of agate inside it. 'It's complicated.'

She searched his face.

'I love my father, Rose. He's not unremittingly awful. When he forgets to nurse his grudges, he can be good company.' He let out a breath slowly. 'I understand why he does what he does. I understand his vulnerabilities, and it makes me ache for him.'

She glanced away.

'All of which is compounded by the fact that

I hate so much of what he says and does. I agree with so few of his opinions and attitudes.'

She glanced back.

'What you're really asking me, though, is if I'd lie to protect him.'

Her mouth fell open—that soft, kissable and surprisingly mischievous mouth.

'The answer is I don't know. Probably… To an extent. There's a line, though, which I won't go beyond.'

'Which is?'

'I won't let him hurt you.'

CHAPTER NINE

LINCOLN'S WORDS ECHOED through Rose. *'I won't let him hurt you.'* She stared at him, moistened her lips.

His face could be carved from granite. 'You have my word.'

The flash in those dark eyes, the way his lips firmed, had things inside her clenching, heating… melting.

Making love with Lincoln had been a revelation. She'd expected pleasure, but she hadn't expected such joy; hadn't known she'd want to throw her arms wide and embrace the world. Or that a lump would lodge in her throat at the sheer beauty of it. She'd never felt closer, more attuned, to another living soul.

Swallowing, she pulled herself up short. That was her inexperience talking. She needed to be careful. In three months this marriage would end and Lincoln would return to Kalku Hills, with the deed to Camels Bridge in his hand.

She couldn't read too much into this, couldn't

let herself fall for him. The horizon turned a soft pink. She *wouldn't* be the silly naïve ingenue.

'You don't believe me?'

Slamming back, she silently cursed herself. Her thoughts should be focussed on securing Garrison Downs' future, nothing more. This thing with Lincoln was temporary, but Garrison Downs was her home, her sisters' home, and she needed to safeguard it for the generations to come.

Lifting her chin, she met his gaze. 'I believe that you don't want your father to hurt me.'

'But?' He placed another rock in her hand— a beautiful deep red. 'Jasper.' He added another. 'Rock crystal.'

She stared at them. 'How do you know the names of them all?'

'When I did my undergraduate degree we were encouraged to study a strand unrelated to our main course. Some people did creative writing, others studied philosophy. I did geology. But back to the subject at hand.'

His father.

'You can't control what your father does. You can probably influence it, but…' She lifted a shoulder, let it drop. 'Which means you can't protect me from the results of his actions, not fully.'

Those large capable hands clenched and unclenched, as if he'd like to take on the world. To protect her?

The thought turned her insides to jelly.

'And the other thing—' Dark eyes met hers and just for a moment she wanted to weep. He looked as solid and steadfast as the ridge of red rock behind them. 'I don't believe you'd choose me over him. You've known and loved him all your life. You've known me for no time at all.'

He nodded, not in agreement but as if he should've realised that this was what she'd think. 'Then that just goes to show how wrong you can be.' He smiled, the creases around his eyes crinkling. 'It's good to know you're not infallible, Rose Waverly.'

Infallible, *her*? Give her a break.

'You said you wanted to bring an end to the bad blood between our families. I want that too. I don't want my children riddled with the same bitterness that my father has fallen victim to. I want my children to be happy and to thrive.'

Children featured in his future?

Her mouth went strangely dry.

'If my father does something to damage Garrison Downs and I support him in that, I will rightfully earn your undying resentment.' Bracing his hands on his knees, he stared at the ground. 'And then this mistrust and the bitterness and the attempts to undermine each other will continue into the future.'

Straightening, he shook his head, placing another pebble in her hand. 'I don't want that.'

That she did believe. Reaching out, she touched

a hand to his cheek. 'Let's do our best to make sure that doesn't happen.'

Everything about him sharpened—determination settling across his features—and then he pulled her into his arms and kissed her with a dizzying intensity that had her dropping all of Ana's pebbles as she wrapped her arms around his neck and tried to climb inside his body.

Before she knew it, they were back at the cabin and falling down onto the mattress, making love with a fierce intensity totally at odds with their earlier slow tenderness. She loved the primal ferocity, loved that he knew exactly what she wanted and how to give it to her. She loved that when he started to slow, to remember her relative inexperience, she could touch him in a certain way, move and clench in a certain way, and his groan would ring in her ears as he flung headlong back into heat and passion.

It made her feel strong and bold.

And then she was undone—begging and crying out his name—more naked than she'd ever been in her life.

Afterwards she lay pressed against his side, her head on his shoulder, his hand trailing lazy circles on her back, her fingers drifting across his stomach.

His hand stilled. 'I have no control where you're concerned. I shouldn't have—'

'Oh, yes, you should.' She glanced up and met those dark eyes. 'I loved every moment of that.'

He grimaced. 'Maybe so, but tomorrow you're going to be sore in places you never even knew you had.'

'Yet I've never felt more physically sated in my life. So if I'm sore tomorrow it'll have been totally worth it.'

He grinned. 'Hungry?'

'Starving.'

They built a fire and when it had died down they cooked potatoes in the embers. Sitting on large flat stones while they waited for them to cook, they opened a bottle of wine, ate cheese, crackers and olives, and then big slices of chocolate cake. They'd meant to save that for afterwards, but they were both too ravenous, and they decided if they wanted to eat dessert before their mains then they could.

Turning the potatoes in the embers, Lincoln glanced across. 'Did you want to continue our earlier conversation? I kind of cut you off.'

In the best possible way, though.

'You still have questions about my father.'

She didn't know if it was a statement or a question. 'Yeah, but...' He raised an eyebrow when she hesitated, and she shrugged. 'I don't want to spoil the mood.' She gestured back behind them. 'What just happened in there... It felt...'

Very slowly he set the barbecue fork down

and moved across to crouch down in front of her. 'What did it feel like?'

She'd promised to be honest. Even when it was hard. *Especially* when it was hard. Pleating the material of the shirt she wore—his shirt—in nerveless fingers, she forced her gaze to his. 'It felt like it meant something.' And then she made herself laugh. 'Listen to me—the naïve little virgin. Throughout the ages women have mistaken physical pleasure to mean something more…a meeting of the souls or—'

'It felt momentous to me, too.'

The very quietness of his words had her heart picking up pace. It startled her how much she wanted to believe him.

You can choose to believe him.

Behind him, crystal stars glittered in a navy sky. She *could* choose to trust him.

Swallowing, she lifted her chin. 'What happened this afternoon felt like a promise.' A promise of what she couldn't really say—a promise of a brighter future, perhaps.

'Yes.' He said the word slowly, as if he felt the truth of that in the depths of himself.

'I don't want to spoil that with talk of your father.' It felt too new, too vulnerable for such realities.

Leaning forward, he pressed a kiss to her brow. 'You and I, we're good, Rose.' He moved back to the fire. 'And talk about our fathers need have no effect on that. So ask your questions.'

Their relationship had shifted today. She hadn't realised making love would have such a momentous impact on *them*. But clearing the air was probably a good idea.

'Does your father really hate us Waverlys?'

He served the potatoes onto two plates and came back to sit on the stone beside her. Balancing their plates on their knees, they broke the potatoes open, slathered them in salt and butter, and waited for them to cool enough to eat.

'You don't understand how much he envied your father or how Holt's success ate away at him. It all escalated after my mother left.' One broad shoulder lifted. 'She was a city woman, like yours. But your mum stayed.'

The legend that was her parents' marriage rose up around them. People might mock it now, discredit it, but there was a solid truth to the love Holt and Rosamund had had for one another. Their marriage hadn't been perfect. But it didn't change the fact that they *had* loved each other.

'It wasn't easy for Mum in the early days. I remember her crying. I remember some dreadful fights.'

She hadn't told anyone other than her sisters about that, but she didn't want him thinking her parents' marriage had been picture perfect. There was the myth and then there was the reality. He'd been so alone, and it mattered. Her heart ached for the young boy he'd been. She'd been so lucky to have her sisters.

'Mum never stopped missing her home. But she stayed, and it made all the difference.' And it had. 'Even though we now know she had a strong reason to leave, she made the decision to stay and fight for her marriage.'

Lincoln's mouth turned grim. 'Mum leaving broke something inside my father. He turned inward and blamed all of his misfortune on Garrison Downs having been lost in that poker game all those years ago. As if there'd been a blight on the family ever since. He believed that if Garrison Downs was his, he'd have all that Holt had—the success, the plaudits of the nation, the family.' He rubbed a hand over his face. 'And just so you know. That day in Marni when you saw him hit me in the general store…'

Her fork of potato halted halfway to her mouth.

'Mum had only been gone a month and what you saw was the culmination of all his fear and frustration. He apologised later. He never hit me again.'

'Good.'

'I dreamed of finding Cordelia's diary when I was a kid because I'd hoped it'd frame the poker game in a way that would…' He shook his head. 'I don't know. Help him come to terms with it all.'

What if it did the opposite, though? What if—?

'My great-grandmother said that the goings-on back then were vastly exaggerated. If she'd lived longer, I'd have eventually known the right questions to ask, but…'

Rose abandoned her food as a growing foreboding grew inside her. 'What are you afraid your father is going to do, Lincoln?' Because it had finally occurred to her that one of the reasons Lincoln was here, one of the reasons he'd agreed to marry her, was to prevent his father from doing something…awful.

Lincoln made a decision in that moment to trust Rose with the truth. What had happened between the two of them this afternoon had changed things. He knew now that he loved this woman. With *all* of himself. He was hers, body and soul. To admit as much, though, would send her scurrying for the hills in a panic. Too much, too soon.

He wouldn't spook her. He'd win her trust, then he'd win her heart. He was smart and resourceful, and she loved making love with him. He *could* make this happen.

Sharing his concerns about his father would help cement the trust growing between them. Lifting a portion of potato to his mouth, he bit into it, letting the warmth and steam rise into his face. He nodded at her plate. 'Eat up, Rose. This is one of the joys of camping out.'

She did as he bid.

He waited until she'd taken a couple of bites before speaking again. 'You ask what I'm worried my father will do. I'm afraid he's going to try and steal some of your cattle.'

Her potato dropped to the ground with a splat. Picking it up, he threw it into the fire, placing the rest of his cooled potato on her plate and reaching for a new one to break open and slather in butter.

'Before you ask, I don't have any solid proof.' He held up a hand. 'And before you say anything, it's not rumour-mongering if it's kept just between ourselves.'

After the briefest of hesitations, she nodded.

'All I have is half a telephone conversation I overheard. All I caught was a truck being arranged to go north on your western boundary.'

'That's the furthest boundary from Kalku Hills.'

It was.

'To divert suspicion that Kalku could be responsible?'

'Possibly.' He ate more potato. 'Or because it's the last area you generally muster. It'd give Clay a chance to get out there undetected.'

'This is why you've been going out in Judy so much. You've been patrolling the boundaries.'

Bingo.

She ate her potato, staring reflectively into the fire. It occurred to him then that one of the reasons he loved her was that she didn't fly into a panic or throw a tantrum or make a drama out of a what-might-happen situation. She really was every bit as cool, calm and measured as she appeared.

Except in bed.

Then she was every inch the passionate, fiery siren.

Maybe she wouldn't panic if you told her you loved her?

His lips cracked into a smile. No, she'd be freaked.

'What are you smiling at?'

He shook himself. 'Your lack of drama. The fact you're not jumping about and waving your arms in a rage.'

'I save that for when things actually happen, not on the off chance that they might. Lincoln, if your dad does this and gets caught, he'll be ruined.'

If he was caught, the fool could go to jail.

'Do you think talking to him would help?'

'I want to say yes, but…' His father had lost all perspective. He wanted to prevent Clay from going too far, from taking a step he'd not be able to come back from. 'If he thought we were onto him, I'm worried he'd just change the plan.'

'And Garrison Downs is big. It's a lot of country to keep an eye on at a time when we're about to be all hands on deck.'

'Yep.'

She stared into the fire. 'Would it help if I gave Kalku Hills access to Camels Bridge now? Early?'

He straightened. 'You'd do that?'

'In an instant if it would help soften things between him and the Waverlys.'

'It'd give him another access point onto your land.'

'We'll be mustering there later in the week. Once we're done, he can drive the cattle through from the north if he wants. I'll let Aaron know as soon as we're back.'

'He might reward your kindness with—'

'Or he might not. But at least I've extended an olive branch. In the meantime, we remain vigilant.' Her gaze returned to the fire. 'Holt was one of the country's leading graziers,' she started slowly.

'He was a legend.'

'And he enjoyed that position, but sometimes, Lincoln, he could've wielded that power with more grace. He enjoyed rubbing his success in your father's face. I know your father needled him every chance he got, but Holt could've ignored it, been the bigger man.'

Rose had worshipped Holt. It was unsettling to hear her criticise him. 'There's a lot of history between our fathers. There'll be things that happened we've no knowledge of.' He glanced down, noted the stubborn jut of her jaw. 'Why are you so angry with him, Rose? Why do you call him Holt now instead of Dad?'

Startled eyes met his. The light from the fire danced across her face, and in that moment her beauty sent a shiver through his heart. If he couldn't make her love him... A weight pressed down on his chest. If he couldn't win her love, life would go on—an endless grey lonely life, a mockery of a life. If this risk didn't pay off, he'd be half a man.

'Is that the personal question you wanted to ask?'

He eased back. 'It's a spur-of-the-moment question. One you don't have to answer.'

Her nose wrinkled, and she refilled their glasses from the bottle of Shiraz.

'If he were here, he'd hate hearing me calling him Holt rather than Dad.' She sipped her wine. 'It's childish, immature, but oddly satisfying.'

He winced. She didn't look particularly satisfied. 'Because of the affair?'

'No.' Those lovely lips turned down. 'Not that I condone what he did. But I remember a period when there were awful fights. Truly awful, Lincoln. I'd have been no more than four or five. Mum wasn't there for a time. But then she returned and things went back to normal.'

Rosamund had left?

'I asked Da— Holt about it a few years ago.'

She might be angry with her father, but he sensed her love for him threading below her words.

'After Tilly was born, Mum had severe post-natal depression.'

The air whistled between his teeth. 'Hell.'

'She'd been uprooted from all that she knew and transplanted into a totally alien—and isolated—world. She had three children in quick succession. On top of that she had to deal with my grand-mother—who wasn't sympathetic to her plight—while Holt spent long hours on the land...sometimes days.'

'That's a lot for anyone to handle.'

'He said it was like she'd changed overnight. She alternated between being withdrawn and then raging at him. He thought she'd gone from loving him to hating him in the space of a few of years. She accused him of ruining her life and—' She broke off, stared at her hands. 'She was hospital-ised with depression for a short time. He thought their marriage was over.'

Linc could barely get his head around what she was telling him. 'I had no idea...' Holt and Rosa-mund had always presented such a united front, had always seemed so deeply in love.

'That they were less than perfect?' She gave a low laugh. 'It's why my view of marriage has never been as rosy as Tilly's. I knew they'd had a rocky patch. I knew Holt had thought the mar-riage was over. I didn't know about the affair.

While I can't condone it, I can understand him seeking solace.'

'Why are you so angry with him, then?'

Her eyes flashed. 'For keeping a sister from us! Ana should never have been hidden away like some dirty little secret. We should've had the chance to know her. She grew up thinking we'd resent and loathe her if we'd known about her. He should've publicly acknowledged her, and she should've had all the same advantages we had growing up.'

Reaching out, he pulled her into his lap, wanting to soothe her agitation. 'But Ana is in your life now and she knows you love her.'

'Yes, but—'

'Rose, your father loved all of you—the fact all four daughters inherit Garrison Downs proves that.'

She folded her arms and glared at him, but she also rested back against him as if she belonged there. 'So you're saying I should just forgive him?'

He traced a finger down her cheek. 'You will forgive him.' Her lips trembled. 'You love him and you'll eventually forgive him just like you'd forgive one of your sisters if they hurt you.'

He stared down at her, aching for her. She'd lost her father, had all she'd known about him turned on its head. It was enough to rattle anyone. 'Did your mother know about Ana?'

Her hair brushed his cheek as she shook her head. 'She knew about the affair, but, according to Ana, Holt and Lili had ended things before they discovered Lili was pregnant.'

'If she'd known he'd had a child to Lili, how would Rosamund have reacted? Would it have been one obstacle too many?'

She glanced up, swallowed.

'It would've devastated you all if Rosamund had given up on Holt and demanded a divorce. It would've torn your family apart.'

Her eyes swirled with confusion, agitation.

'It's only natural Holt would want to save Rosamund from further pain. He would've done just about anything to keep your family together. That's understandable.'

She frowned. 'But—'

'And Ana had Lili. There would never have been any question of Ana coming to live at Garrison Downs. She'd have remained with her mum. Holt was financially responsible for her. He didn't abandon her.'

'No, but—'

'You had a wonderful childhood with your parents and sisters. Clearly your parents' marriage emerged even stronger.'

'Well, yes, but—'

'And Ana has had a good life with her mum.'

'Of course! Lili is wonderful.'

'Holt had to know that the news would hurt

you. But maybe the hurt you're suffering now is the lesser hurt than if your family had been broken apart.'

'But what about the hurt Ana has suffered?'

It was a wail in the night and he tucked her hair behind her ear. 'It's easy to rewrite the past into the shape we want for it, but if your parents had divorced and you'd been forced to spend half your time in England with your mum and half here at Garrison Downs—your lives completely upended—isn't it possible you'd have felt some resentment towards Ana?'

He pressed a finger to her lips when she opened her mouth.

'The scenario in your mind is one in which everyone is acting as their ideal best selves. All I'm saying is that the reality might have been different. And the fact is, you can't change the past. All you can do is make the best of your present.'

'Hmph. Why do you have to sound so reasonable?'

'I don't like seeing you tied up in knots. You deserve to be happy.'

She glanced down at her hands. 'I've been lucky, I know. I've an embarrassment of riches when it comes to family. I've no right to complain.'

'Your dad betrayed your trust, and, while I don't doubt he regretted it, you've every right to feel hurt and let down. But, Rose, don't forget that a mistake—even a big one—doesn't mean he wasn't a good man. It doesn't mean all of your memories of him are a lie. It doesn't mean everything you thought of him is a lie.'

The inherent truth of Lincoln's words seeped into Rose in a slow trickle. She moistened her lips. Some of the things she knew about her father were still true. 'He was a good cattleman.' Her heart thudded. 'And a good businessman.'

'One of the best.'

In her mind's eye she saw Holt on Jasper, the black stallion cutting behind a mob of cattle, man and horse moving as one. Momentarily removing his hat to swipe an arm across his brow, he caught her eye, winked and grinned, looking every inch the legend he was.

Her throat thickened. 'He was a good dad to Evie, Tilly and me.' He'd taught them to ride, to swim, to navigate home by the stars. He'd encouraged them to follow their dreams, had wrapped them in his love.

She gave a sudden sob. He'd hurt her. He should never have kept Ana a secret from them. But he hadn't kept Ana a secret forever—he'd sent Ana to them, had made sure Garrison Downs was hers too. It hadn't all been a lie.

Lincoln pulled her against his chest and let her cry. One large hand stroking her hair.

The storm was brief, but cleansing. 'Thank you,' she whispered. 'I feel as if I have my dad back.'

'I only told you what you already know in your own heart.'

She lifted her head to meet his gaze, glancing beyond him to the star-jewelled sky. Pushing off his lap, she disappeared inside the cabin, returning a moment later with a couple of blankets. 'Have you ever made love beneath a starry sky beside a campfire?'

'Is that what you'd like to do?'

'More than life itself.'

He took the blankets from her and kissed her deeply. 'Your wish is my command.'

CHAPTER TEN

TWO DAYS AT the waterhole with Lincoln weren't anywhere near enough, but the muster couldn't be delayed any longer. They packed up camp, and Lincoln dangled the car keys from his fingers. 'May I?'

At her nod, he held the passenger door open for her as if she were a queen, saw her seated, and then he negotiated the rustic track with an unhurried ease that had her shifting in her seat and wishing...

What? That they could've stayed at the waterhole forever?

She focussed on the scenery instead. Thanks to the past year's record rainfall, native grasses stretched away in all directions, waves of gold bending in a soft breeze. She loved it—all of it. The dry dusty plains to the west, the pockets of Eucalypt forests beside the river, the lushness surrounding the lakes, the flinty red hills. She even loved the red dust that settled on one's hair and eyelashes.

Yet none of it could distract her from the man beside her. He was beautiful. He made love beautifully. He *had* made her scream. He'd also made her beg, sigh, laugh…and a couple of times he'd damn near made her cry.

She was sore in places she'd never known she had. But it was a good sore—the same as after a hard day in the saddle, wrangling cattle. And it didn't dampen the desire rushing through her now. She wondered if she'd ever get enough of him.

It's called a honeymoon phase for a reason.

And yet she couldn't imagine the intensity fading.

Naïve little virgin.

'Do you know I haven't asked my personal question yet?'

Lincoln's words had her crashing back. He hadn't?

'Guess I had other things on my mind.'

His lazy grin heated her blood.

'Wanna ask it now?'

He nodded. 'You mentioned that one unexpected pregnancy in the family was enough— referring, I suppose, to Eve and Nate. How would you feel if we did become unexpectedly pregnant?'

The *we* surprised her, but she appreciated it too.

'Not sure I expect an answer. It's probably not something you've considered. But if the idea horrifies you…'

Her stomach performed a slow forward roll—not of horror, but of longing. Her mouth dried at the pictures that played through her mind.

Dear God. She couldn't have those kinds of longings with this man. While she couldn't imagine ever tiring of making love with him, she wasn't foolish enough to believe the feeling was mutual. He might no longer be the playboy the district considered him, but it didn't mean he was ready to settle down.

'I like kids,' he continued, 'and I very much want some of my own eventually. You?'

She had to swallow before she could speak. 'I always figured they'd feature in my future.'

'If we had a child, Rose, it would change things.'

'Understatement much, Lincoln?' She laughed, but absurdly she wanted to cry.

'I don't want to be a part-time father. And from what you just said, I'm guessing you wouldn't want to be a part-time mother.'

No! She wanted her child—children—growing up with her. She stared at that hard, lean profile and suddenly blinked. 'Are you saying that if we became pregnant, you'd want to remain married?'

He looked at her then, those dark eyes briefly blazing. He didn't say anything, just gave a hard nod.

Her stomach clenched. Her chest clenched. And

somewhere lower down clenched too. *Don't be absurd.* The idea was too ridiculous for words.

'I don't want you thinking I'm going to be lax with contraception. I mean to be careful. But no method is a hundred per cent effective. So if the idea of an unplanned pregnancy appals you, you might want to consider an additional form of contraception besides condoms.' He shrugged. 'You might want to anyway. In an ideal world, a planned pregnancy is best.'

And yet his tone almost implied the opposite— that an unplanned pregnancy wouldn't appal him.

He flicked a glance at her when she remained silent. 'Didn't mean to freak you out.'

'Not freaked out.' *Liar.*

'Just figured it was something we should consider.'

'Absolutely.' He deserved more from her, though. He'd raised a difficult topic and had been startlingly honest. 'The situation you just described doesn't appal me, Lincoln. But you're right, it's not ideal.' No matter how much it might tempt her.

He raised an eyebrow as if aware there was something she wasn't saying.

'I'd hate to trap you in a marriage that wasn't your idea, and not what you wanted.'

He grinned. 'It might not have been my idea, but it was a good one, Rose. I'm enjoying it so far.'

She couldn't help but laugh. 'I'll make a tele health appointment this week.'

Reaching across, he took her hand and squeezed it, rested it against his thigh. Ahead of them, three emus raced off to the right on long, gangly legs. Emus were considered a symbol of survival and adaptability. And maybe that was what she and Lincoln would do—adapt and survive. The thought had her lips lifting.

For the next three weeks, it was all hands on deck as they mustered in the station's south-eastern corner—the boundary closest to Clay Garrison and Kalku Hills. Rose kept her eyes peeled for signs of unusual activity, but nothing raised alarm bells. Nevertheless, she heaved a sigh of relief when they had the cattle vaccinated, ear-tagged, and those going to market on trucks and rumbling off to the sale yards.

Every evening, Lincoln checked in with Jackson, the Kalku Hills stockman, to find out how things were going next door. Clay had gone quiet. She didn't know if she ought to be worried or not.

But each night, regardless of how hard they'd worked during the day, she and Lincoln made love. Apparently they were never too tired for that.

Mustering eighteen thousand head of cattle across fifteen thousand square kilometres would take a full three months, and yet Rose was careful to ensure her staff had rest days. She didn't want fatigue causing accidents or mishaps.

'You mind if I head over to Kalku?' Lincoln asked during one set of rest days.

'Of course not.' And yet something inside her sank.

'They're mustering a tricky bit of terrain and the helicopter pilot has come down with appendicitis.'

'Ouch.' Kalku Hills was Lincoln's home. Of course he wanted to help. 'You're free to spend your time however you want, Lincoln. You don't have to help here with the muster if you'd prefer to be at Kalku.'

'I *want* to be here.'

For now. But in three months' time—*two* months' time, she amended. When their agreement had been fulfilled, Lincoln *would* return to Kalku. She'd be a fool to forget it.

'It's the first time Dad has asked anything of me since...'

Since they'd married? She nodded.

'And I want to check that everything is as it should be over there.'

She and Lincoln were consolidating a new working relationship they could take forward into the future. She had absolutely no reason not to trust him.

'You be careful out there,' was all she said.

'Always. But tomorrow night I'll be challenging you to another game of chess. Hopefully this time we can finish it.'

That had her grinning. 'I'll look forward to it.'

* * *

The following afternoon, the sound of Lincoln's plane landing shook Rose from the torpor of having sat too long with the accounts. Today she'd faced her demons. After their conversation about Holt at the waterhole, it had felt like time—time to stop avoiding the office, to claim it as her own and start working in it rather than grabbing her laptop and the accounts and settling elsewhere in the house.

Lincoln believed in her. The district's fears had eased. She hadn't messed up. And while it still felt too soon to take over the running of such a massive operation, this was her home, her legacy... and she had a vision for Garrison Downs' future. She *could* do it.

Seating herself behind the desk, she'd thought she might feel awed or a fraud...burdened by all she'd found herself responsible for. But she placed the piece of amber that Lincoln had given her all of those years ago on the desk, alongside the glass horse—named Peridot—that Tilly had sent her from Chaleur, and the silver pen that had been her twenty-first birthday gift from Evie. Touching her tiger's eye bracelet for luck, she set to work. And once she started, she became lost to the work and was ridiculously productive.

She'd felt as if her mother had been sitting in her chair by the window, her love and pride reaching out to her daughter, her quiet strength bolstering Rose's own resilience. At her back she'd felt a presence too—Holt—not intimidating or intrusive, just *encouraging*. She felt, for the briefest of moments, as if she had the very best of both her parents.

In that moment she'd realised she carried that inside her—that she would always have it. A weight had lifted and she'd cried, but the tears had been a release. They'd allowed happy memories to surface—her mother's smile, her father's laugh. Christmas as a child with her sisters, bouncing and excited. Family dinners. Picnics. Bedtime stories.

She wanted to tell Lincoln about it all.

Maybe he'd like a cold beer by the pool?

Or she could join him in the shower, perhaps...

Standing and stretching, she lost herself in that scenario until she glimpsed his tall broad form sauntering through the gums at the edge of the garden. When he halted and glanced to his right, she craned her neck to see what he was looking at.

After the briefest of hesitations, he set his footsteps in that direction. Stepping out onto the veranda, she started after him, wanting to know what had caught his attention. Blossom followed at her heels, her nails clicking on the veranda's tessellated tiles.

Lincoln had passed through the garden and now started up the low rise in the direction of the old settler's cottage. She opened her mouth to call out to him, but closed it again. What had he seen?

You mean, what is he up to?

'Grandma,' she murmured, 'if I want your opinion I'll ask for it.'

Her eyes narrowed. There was something almost furtive about his movements that had a chill settling across her scalp. Topping the rise, she watched in silence as he ducked straight inside the cottage. Her heart pounded. Probably due to the stories Pop had told her about the giant brown snake that used to live there.

Lincoln was up to something. Acid burned her stomach. And she knew exactly what it was—he was hoping to find Cordelia's diary. Why would he do that behind her back?

With a single gesture she sent Blossom behind the cottage out of sight, before creeping up to one of the two windows. Inside, Lincoln checked the walls and rafters. Ducking down when his gaze turned in her direction, she crept across to the other window. When she peeked in again, she found him crouching down and running his fingers along a row of stones as if… Was he counting?

His fingers halted, and even from where she stood she heard his quick intake of breath. Prising a stone loose, he lowered it to the ground. Nestled in the gap behind lay something wrapped in calf leather, tied with a piece of knotted cord. Reaching in, he took it out and blew the dust from it, staring at it reverently before placing it carefully beneath his shirt.

Tiptoeing around the corner, she flattened herself against the wall. His footsteps faded as he strode back towards the homestead, the afternoon shadows lengthening. She didn't emerge until he was out of sight.

Why hadn't he told her he'd worked out where the diary was? And what the hell did he think was in it? Spots danced at the edges of her vision. Had she been a fool to trust him?

Bracing her hands on her knees against a wave of nausea, she pulled air into cramped lungs. He'd said he'd wanted to find the diary to help Clay come to terms with the past. She had no reason not to believe him.

'Stop being obtuse, Rose. That diary could damn Louisa May. And if it does—'

She tried to block out her grandmother's voice. Even if it did, the land had been in Waverly hands for the last hundred and twenty years. It was the Waverly family who had made Garrison Downs what it was.

If Lincoln wasn't trying to make mischief, though, why hadn't he shared the treasure hunt adventure with her? She covered her face with her hands. Had he slept with her simply to throw her off the scent? Had he been searching all this time while her back had been turned?

Blossom whined and nosed her leg. Crouching down, Rose buried her face in her fur. Eventually she straightened, faced what needed to be faced. Lincoln had been playing her for a fool. *She* had been a sentimental fool.

She took the shortest route home. She'd been naïve and now she needed to work out what the hell to do. She headed straight into the office.

'Afternoon, Rose.'

She slammed to a halt. Lincoln sat in the chair on the other side of the desk, grinning that grin she should never have allowed herself to believe in, but even now it had things inside her softening.

Nausea churned.

Don't throw up.

She couldn't let him see how badly his betrayal affected her. She couldn't…

Stumbling around the desk, she sat. She'd ask him to leave. Tonight. *Right now.* And she wouldn't ask—*she'd order.*

She opened her mouth, refusing to look at him, staring instead at her hands as she flattened them on the desk. 'Lincoln…'

She blinked. Directly in front of her sat a leather roll tied with cord, the cord still knotted and intact. She stared at it and then at him. He *hadn't* taken it. He *hadn't* hidden it. He *wasn't* a wretched, black-hearted traitor.

'Tut-tut. Boots in the house? I'm shocked, Rose Waverly.'

Her mind had blanked. She tried to find her way back to the surface. 'Holt's office, his rules.'

'Your office now. Your rules. Which are?'

'Boots allowed. In here. Not the rest of the house.'

His grin widened at her choppy sentences.

She pointed at the leather pouch. 'Is that…?'

'Cordelia's diary? I'm hoping so.'

He hadn't stolen it, hadn't hidden it away. Her vision blurred. He wasn't hoping it contained something that would take her home from her.

She couldn't move. She could only stare from the leather pouch to him and back again. 'But… *how*?'

'My father is still being pig-headed. Which irritated me more than usual today. Got me thinking about the diary again. And when I was flying in, I saw the old settler's cottage and wondered—what if those old tales weren't referring to the original homestead but to the original *dwelling*?'

A deliciously broad shoulder lifted. 'While we've been on muster, I've been trying to remember everything Gran told me. She said I shouldn't believe what everyone said about Louisa May… and something about *three up and six across*. Like it was some private joke. Today, when I flew over the cottage, I realised it was a direction.'

He *had* been counting!

'Three stones up—'

'And six across.' And here the treasure was, right in front of her. She'd been right to trust him.

The relief hit her like a punch, pulling her from her daze. Rather than reaching for the calfskin parcel, though, she shot around the desk to fling herself into his arms.

'Whoa! I—'

But her mouth had claimed his, fierce and possessive. He kissed her back with the same intensity, breaking off to gasp when her hands tugged the hem of his shirt from his jeans to flatten against the hard flat planes of his stomach. 'Rose, I—'

Dragging him to his feet, she led him to the sofa and pushed him down. 'Want me to stop?'

He shook his head.

She closed the French doors. She locked the office door. His eyes blazed when she turned back to face him. Standing in front of him, she undressed—slowly and seductively, like some soap-opera starlet—but it worked because his breathing grew more and more ragged.

'Rose, you're killing me.'

And then she proceeded to make love to him with her hands, her mouth, her body—telling him in a language that needed no words how much she admired him, how much she desired him…how much she *liked* him.

But then there were no more thoughts—just sensation. Glorious sensation.

Afterwards, when they could move again, she lifted her head from where it was pressed against his neck. She'd straddled him and she should probably move and give the poor guy a chance to breathe again. His hand on her waist stilled her. With his other hand, he lifted her chin until liquid dark eyes bored into hers. 'Did something happen today? Anything I should know?'

She cupped his face, let her hands drift down to enjoy the strength of his neck, before sending him a straight-from-the-heart smile—one she couldn't have contained if she'd wanted to. 'Only that I missed you.'

Something flared in his eyes, and she thought it might be hope. Maybe both of them were becoming more invested in this temporary marriage than they'd meant to. The thought should terrify her.

Instead she recalled his earlier words about his father being difficult and a hard determination settled in her chest. This man had never had a proper family of his own, not one who loved him unconditionally—not a warm, loving, sharing family. But she could give him a taste of that now. She could share what she had with him.

Something in Rose's face made Lincoln's heart beat harder. The way she'd made love to him just now...

She'd made him feel *cherished*. He searched

her face. The light in her eyes…the smile on her lips… Was she starting to care? Something fierce and fiery rushed through him.

He ground back the declaration pressing against his throat. It was too soon to tell her he loved her. They had time. He wouldn't spook her.

'What?' he asked instead as she continued to survey him.

Easing off his lap, she started hauling on her clothes, grinning at him over her shoulder. She pointed at the leather pouch on the desk. 'Family conference in thirty minutes.'

He stilled. Except his heart, which thudded like a wild thing.

'Ever since we Waverly sisters have heard about it, we've been dying to know what's in that diary.'

She was including him in that inner circle? He'd finally get a peek behind the curtain and be a part of the family that had enthralled him his whole life? He opened his mouth but not a single sound emerged.

'Chop-chop.' She clapped her hands. 'You need to make yourself respectable. I messed up your pretty hair.'

That had him grinning. Speaking of messed hair…

She turned on her phone and sang the first line of Sister Sledge's 'We Are Family'.

'Girls,' she dictated into the phone, 'Lincoln is the man of the hour. He's found the diary. I'm opening it in thirty minutes. You know what to do if you don't want to miss it.'

He heard the pings as her sisters all immediately answered. They sounded like excitement and love and belonging.

Thirty minutes later he was seated behind the desk next to Rose. Eve and Nate sat on the sofa at right angles to them. At Rose's insistence that Eve have the most comfortable seat in the house, he and Nate had moved it. Up on the giant screen on the back wall, Matilda and Prince Henri appeared in one window, and Ana and Connor in another.

Matilda squealed when she saw everyone and immediately blew kisses. Ana waved, her shy smile broad.

'Show me my future niece,' Matilda demanded.

Eve rose and smoothed a hand over her stomach with a big grin and soft eyes. 'Isn't she beautiful?'

'Gorgeous!'

Coos and excited murmurings filled the air. Matilda danced in her seat, clapping her hands, Ana shot so far forward that Connor slipped an arm around her waist to stop her from falling off her chair, while Rose just grinned. The broadness of her smile and the way her eyes shone made his breath catch. *This.* This was what he wanted.

Nate caught his eye and winked.

Matilda sobered and pointed. 'Rose, I hope

you're making sure she's not overdoing it, that she's taking it easy.'

'Nate is taking perfect care of her.'

'Cross my heart.' Nate lifted a hand and crossed his heart, the tattoos on his forearm endearingly at odds with the quaint gesture.

'Pfft, Eve won't listen to you. But Rose, now... she's the Boss.'

Lincoln glanced at Rose, but her father's old nickname only made her grin.

'We're all terrified of her when she's on the warpath.'

'And we all know that's a load of old cobblers, but I *am* going to call this meeting to order.' And with that Rose held up the leather roll. It was the first time she'd touched it and it was as if the very air stilled as all eyes turned to stare at it.

'Tilly, you're the expert. How should we do this?' She lifted the pouch closer to the camera.

Matilda bent down, gestured for Rose to turn it over. 'The leather is in good condition, but that cord...' She shook her head. 'The historian in me is urging you to pack it up and send it to me. If I can't get hold of the right equipment to protect and date it, I know people who can.'

'You always were a comedian, Tilly,' Eve trilled. 'You know that's not going to happen. Those in favour of opening the roll here and now, raise your hands.'

Rose and Eve both raised their hands.

'Ana?' Rose kept her voice gentle.

Ana squirmed. 'Sorry, Tilly, but I'm dying to know.' She raised her hand as well.

'No need to apologise, Ana Banana.' Matilda raised her hand too. 'Me four. Just, Rose…try and be gentle.'

Rose glanced at Lincoln. 'As Lincoln is the one who found it, and as it probably belongs to his great-great-grandmother, perhaps he should do the honours.'

'What, with these big lugs?' He held his hands up, shaking his head. 'No, you have at it, Rose.'

Settling the pouch in front of her, she took a deep breath and did her best to gently unknot the cord, but it promptly disintegrated.

'Don't throw it!' Matilda wrung her hands. 'It can be used to help date the package.'

Rifling through the desk drawers, Rose emerged triumphant with a Ziploc bag, which made her sister laugh. 'Dad always had a collection of those on hand for my discoveries.'

After the cord had been carefully stowed inside the bag, Rose gently unrolled the pouch. Inside was a package of…

'Letters,' Rose said, pulling them out. 'Not a diary. Letters addressed to Cordelia Garrison…'

His ancestor.

She turned the top one over. 'From Lissy May.'

'Louisa May,' Eve and Matilda breathed at the same time.

'And some addressed to Louisa May from Cordelia too.'

'Read them, Rose!'

That burst from Ana, but both Eve and Matilda nodded.

CHAPTER ELEVEN

ROSE CAREFULLY SHUFFLED through the letters. Lincoln's gaze caught on those fingers, recalled the feel of them on his overheated flesh in this very room earlier, and had to swallow.

'This one is dated first and it's from Louisa May. *"Dear Cordelia, A poker match? A poker match! I nearly fainted when Elinor Conklin informed me that the town was agog with the news that I'd won Garrison Downs from you in a poker match. She said she'd had the words direct from the horse's mouth—you—so that there was no use me trying to deny it. You'd have been proud of how I rose to the occasion. I shrugged and asked her if she'd like to be invited to our next game. You've never seen anyone make their excuses quicker. She hightailed away as if I was the most wicked of women. I had a hearty laugh afterwards, but seriously you should've warned me. To my surprise, rather than making me persona non gratis, it appears that my standing in the community has risen in some circles. Miss Delia*

Gray, who's so high in the instep, deigned to stop and ask after my brother when I was in town yesterday. And, yes, Michael's health is improving, thanks to your kindness. And reports of our wild deeds do not appear to have scared Ned Waverly away as the dear man continues to pay me court. Is it wrong of me to hope that soon I shall be Mrs Edward Waverly? I'm sure it's most unladylike, but you know what they say—as soon as a woman turns to gambling she loses all decorum. But seriously, I implore you, dearest Cordelia, to accept the deeds back to Garrison Downs as soon as you're sure we've scared off Geoffrey Bannister, as that is, I believe, your design in starting such a rumour. I can imagine the difficulties Arthur is now making for you too. Much love, your faithful friend, Lissy May."'

Rose set the letter down. 'They weren't enemies. They were *friends*.'

'Not just friends,' Eve said, 'but besties.'

'Sisters of the heart,' Ana breathed.

Matilda stared at the letters as if she ached to hold them for herself. 'There *wasn't* a poker match.'

Apparently that was a rumour started by his great-great-grandmother.

'Oh, hurry.' Matilda groaned. 'Read the next one.'

Rose picked up a second letter. 'This one's from Cordelia. *"Dearest Lissy, How I wish I could've seen your face when Elinor told you of our iniquitous deeds. Don't be too cross with me. I was in the process of writing to you when your letter came. I did not think you would be going to town for another six weeks at least and believed that I, thus, would have time to tell you what was afoot. However, let's get to the heart of the matter. Garrison Downs is yours, my dear friend, and there's nothing my dreadful brother Arthur can do about it—regardless of how he might bellyache and complain around the district that I've ruined him. He squandered his own inheritance from Grandfather, and I won't allow him to squander mine. As you well know, Papa not only owns Kalku Hills, but vast swathes of land to the north-east. I am far from destitute. I repeat: Garrison Downs is yours, my dear. Not only have you saved my life three times, but Arthur has done you and Michael a grave disservice. My conscience won't rest easy until amends are made. I know that if I should ever need a place of refuge in the future, I will always find one with you at Garrison Downs. Now, let me tell you the colour Geoffrey Bannister's face turned when he heard the news and came knocking on my door to demand I refute such dastardly rumours. First it turned puce, and then the most interesting shade of purple, and then a sickly shade of yellow. It really was most fascinating to witness. He informed me that I am a wicked wanton with no regard for my future, my children's future or any respect for God Almighty himself. What woman would want to lumber herself with such a proselytising prig of a husband? I ask you. But he will never again darken my door—his words, not mine—and I cannot tell you the weight that has lifted from me. While he wears the face of a Christian, underneath he is a sadistic brute and I'm heartily relieved to be rid of him. Now I plan to woo my Thomas properly and convince him to make an honest woman of me.'''*

Rose set the letter down carefully, stared at her sisters.

'I want to know how Louisa May saved Cordelia's life three times.' Matilda rested her chin in her palm. 'I bet there was a brown snake involved at least once.'

There were a lot of ways to die out here. Even more back then.

'Nursed her through a fever?' Ana offered. 'Jumped into a swollen river and saved her from drowning?'

Eve snorted. 'Went to stay with her to save her from boredom?'

A laugh burst from Rose. 'You're right, this pair are a riot.'

'I wonder what disservice Arthur did to Lissy and Michael, though?'

'The brother sounds like a piece of work, and

Geoffrey Bannister sounds even worse.' Rose picked up the next letter. 'Shall I continue?'

Rose read letters that detailed Cordelia's marriage to Thomas Sinclair, a lowly station hand, and how her father gifted Kalku Hills to the couple when Thomas agreed to take Garrison as his surname.

'No way.' Linc leaned forward, and she showed him the line in the letter. He eased back, grinning. 'Wait till my father hears about that.'

Her eyes danced before returning to the letters. They revealed that Louisa May married Edward Waverly and that they settled at Garrison Downs. It became clear that in the early days of their marriages, the two women relied on each other enormously.

When Cordelia gave birth to *'a bonny son'*, Louisa May and Ned were named godparents. As a gift to her new godson, Louisa May had a codicil attached to her will stating that if there were no Waverly sons to inherit Garrison Downs, and if the Waverly daughters were all unmarried, then the station would pass back to the Garrison family.

Rose sat back as if the air had been punched from her body.

'She didn't do it to punish us!' Eve burst out. 'She did it out of respect for her dearest friend and for the godson she loved. And because Cordelia had gifted it to her in the first place.'

'She adds here that the two of them know how hard it is for women on the land alone, and that she hopes all of their daughters find husbands as fine as their fathers, and that their sons should find wives with the love for the land that she and Cordelia have.' Rose shrugged. 'And that's it.'

They were all silent for a moment.

'They weren't enemies.' Rose swung to him, her eyes shining. 'They were besties.'

He couldn't stop from reaching out and touching her cheek. His heart swelled. 'Friends,' he murmured.

'Ooh, you two are making bedroom eyes at each other,' Matilda cooed.

Rose dragged her gaze from his. 'Shut up, Button.'

It made everyone laugh, and then she rose and scanned each of the letters, and sent copies to her sisters…and to him. She and Matilda discussed how best to get the letters to Chaleur for Matilda to verify them. None of them doubted that the letters were real, but official authentication would provide authority for this new version of the station's history.

He suspected Rose wanted that for him. He'd be able to take that back to his father, and maybe then Clay would finally look to the future instead of remaining mired in the past.

A new history. Friends. Not enemies. No poker match. No lying or cheating. Cordelia had gifted land that was legitimately hers to her dearest friend, and the two women had been each other's chief support. Sisters of the heart, as Ana had said. They'd been family.

And to be here now like this, in the middle of the Waverly clan, accepted as part of the family, he realised what a treasure that was. His father had wasted his life in bitterness. Lincoln wasn't making the same mistake. After today's revelations he was only more determined to make Rose his own.

They made love again that night, and Rose gazed into his eyes the entire time, let him see her most secret self, unedited—the awe, the ecstasy—as if she wanted there to be no secrets between them, as if she was trusting him with her very essence. It left him wanting to kiss her feet.

Afterwards they lay side by side as they waited for their hearts to stop racing and their breathing to slow.

'That was…'

She nodded. 'It was.'

He turned his head on the pillow to find her watching him. 'Okay?' he asked gently.

Was she rocked by the intensity of their lovemaking, worried that it was one-sided? He could put her mind at rest on that—

'I have a confession to make.' She rolled to fully face him.

He turned to face her too, his senses sharpening.

'I owe you an apology. I saw you heading for the old settler's cottage this afternoon and I followed you.'

He frowned. 'Why didn't you call out? We could've searched together.'

She glanced down, moistened her lips. 'Your manner seemed…odd. Almost furtive.'

He pushed up into a sitting position, resting back against the headboard. His temples pounded. Would she never trust him?

She sat up too. 'Why didn't you come and get me so we could make the discovery together?'

'It felt like a long shot. I didn't want to get my hopes up.'

She pleated the sheet between her fingers. 'When you found those letters…'

He covered her hand with his own. 'You thought I meant to keep them from you?'

'I went into instant melodramatic soap-opera mode, thinking they must contain something that painted Louisa May in a bad light, and that the only reason you married me was to get your hands on them.'

Her words shouldn't rake his soul so raw. She knew now she'd been mistaken, but a sick realisation had bile rising in his throat. 'If I hadn't placed them on your desk when I did…'

She nodded, her face pale. 'I'm sorry.'

He'd wanted to play the hero for her, to bring

home the prize so she'd think him wonderful. Instead, he'd nearly wrecked everything.

'When I thought you meant to betray me, I was gutted.'

He stilled, a pulse ticcing to life. 'You were upset?'

She lifted her eyes to his and he saw the shadows stretching through them. 'I thought we'd become friends.' One slim shoulder lifted. 'More than friends, actually.'

Her openness, her vulnerability, stole his breath. 'Rose…sweetheart.'

'And the thought of losing that left me bereft.'

'You haven't lost it.'

'When I realised my mistake, I was so relieved and so elated.'

She cared.

The knowledge hit him sure and swift.

She cared.

It might not be love. But, like trust, given time it could grow.

'You didn't have to tell me any of that. Why did you?'

'We promised to be honest with each other.'

And she was a woman of her word.

'I figure that's especially important when it's hard.' Her fingers fluttered about her throat. 'If I could be that mistaken about your actions, it made me realise you could be mistaken about mine. It made me realise how careful we need to be. The trust is growing, but it's still in its infancy.'

From now on, he needed to make sure that all of his actions were transparent, that she wasn't in danger of misreading him. But…

His chest grew lighter, bigger.

She cared.

'Rose, I've been thinking. We could extend the length of our marriage beyond three months if we wanted.'

Blue eyes searched his. 'You don't think you'll be sick of me by then?'

She said it as a joke, but he didn't laugh. 'You want to know why I really married you?'

Her eyes widened.

'Because I've always *liked* you, always been drawn to you. I wanted a chance to get to know you. I've never felt for any woman what I feel for you. I wanted to know where, if anywhere, that might lead.'

Her mouth fell open.

'And maybe the relationship between us has an end date, but, as far as I'm concerned, it's not looming on my horizon any time soon. I, for one, would like to see where it could take us.'

He could've groaned out loud when she moistened her lips. 'Maybe…' Her voice was a croak. She cleared her throat and started again. 'Maybe when the mustering is done, you and I could go away somewhere for a week or two.'

Then she smiled and adrenaline pumped through him, his heart soaring light and free. She was open to exploring what was developing between them. She *cared*.

CHAPTER TWELVE

ROSE PAUSED TO admire the sight of Lincoln and
Thunder pivoting, wheeling to the right and then
galloping to cut off a breakaway mob, directing
them back to the main herd. Strong thighs flex-
ing, spine and shoulders fluid, horse and rider
moving as one.

Lincoln looked good on a horse. Seriously good.
There weren't many who could boast horseman-
ship to rival Holt's, but Lincoln was one of them.

He's a good lad.

She smiled.

Yeah, but I bet Grandma's having conniptions.

Her father's laughter sounded through her,
and she found herself grinning. Then someone
shouted, 'Left flank!' and she and Opal spun into
action.

The past month had been insanely busy—
muster always was—but it had been heaven too.
She loved this time of year. Mustering might be
back-breaking work, but few things could beat
being out under a peerless sky on Opal, bring-

ing the cattle into the yards. *This* was where she belonged.

The other place she belonged, apparently, was in Lincoln's arms—when the sun had gone down and the stars had come out and the world had hushed and shrunk to just the two of them.

He turned to grin at her now and she grinned back, knowing he loved all of this as much as she did. From the corner of her eye she saw Aaron scowl, but ignored him. Aaron had stopped openly challenging her every decision, but she sensed rebellion lurking still beneath the surface.

They ushered the cattle into the giant yard, dust swirling all around. Then began the back-breaking work of drafting the cattle—calves for ear-tagging into one of the smaller yards, others for health checks and vaccinations into another, and those for the sale yards in yet another.

When the calves were done, she leaned down from Opal's back, to unlatch the gate and let them back into the main yard to find their mothers, backing Opal up first so the two of them would be out of the way of the stamping rush of hooves. She was dying for a cup of tea, and as soon as this was done they could stop for half an hour.

All around dust swirled, the air filled with the lowing of cattle. As she pulled her arm back, her bracelet—the one Ana had made—caught on the sleeve of her shirt, and the sudden wrench sent it flying through the air to land in the red dirt.

Her sister bracelet!

For two tenths of a second she considered leaping off Opal and trying to retrieve it, but the cattle were starting to move and she'd never be able to hold back the panicked press of bodies. With eyes burning—*her precious bracelet*—she eased Opal away.

And then Lincoln was there, dashing across the yard, flinging himself through the space with a speed that had her jaw dropping before fear kicked in. A tiny corner of her brain marvelled that a man as large as Lincoln could move with such speed, but mostly her heart lodged in her throat pounding so hard it hurt.

He'd be trampled!

Injured!

Her stomach gave a sick kick. Or worse.

One long arm swooped down to sweep up her bracelet. A fraction of a moment later a heifer barrelled through where he'd been, but then he took the hand she held out to him and vaulted onto the back of Opal behind her. She cantered them away, Johnno opening the main gate to let them through, slamming it behind them.

Her heart rate would never return to normal. *Never!*

The moment she brought Opal to a halt they both leapt from her back.

With a lazy, laconic grin that sent fury surging through her veins, Lincoln dangled the bracelet from his fingers. Red mist burst behind her eyeballs and she thumped his chest, and then she did it again because it seemed a better idea than bursting into tears. Though she doubted he even felt her blows—he remained unmovable. But while he might think himself indestructible, he wasn't!

'Whoa, Rose.' He held his hands up. 'Rose, I—'

'What the hell were you thinking?' she shouted, gesturing at the yards. 'You could've been injured. Or worse!' He could've died and it made her break into a cold sweat, had her fury redoubling. 'That was the stupidest, most idiotic—'

She broke off to wheel away and press her palms to her eyes.

'But I wasn't hurt.' His voice was low and steady, as if he were talking to a spooked horse. 'I know what that bracelet means to you.'

She spun back, stabbed a finger at him. 'It's not worth your life. It's not worth *anyone's* life.'

'I know what I'm capable of. I took a calculated risk. I knew I could scoop it up and get to safety before too many had come through the gate.'

She wanted to scream. Dragging her hands through her hair, she retied her ponytail, scraping it back hard and tight. 'One miscalculation and you'd have been a pile of broken bones, and the rest of us would've had to risk our necks to save you.'

His head rocked back.

She loved the sense of having Ana near—of

having all her sisters near—but she'd been an idiot to wear the bracelet during muster. 'I don't need a hero, Lincoln. I need someone with a cool head who makes sensible decisions.'

He could have lost his life.

Clicking her tongue to Opal, who immediately trotted over, Rose was back in the saddle in one smooth motion. The rest of the crew had studiously turned their backs to them, and she winced. She shouldn't have raked Lincoln down in front of everyone like that. So much for the cool head she was known for. But if Lincoln had been hurt…

She glanced at him. He'd paled and his face had shuttered. He stared at her with a coldness she didn't recognise. Her hands shook. She'd yelled at him the same way Clay had done. She shouldn't have—

He could've been killed!

Opal danced sideways as Rose's hands tightened on the reins. She took advantage of the moment to soothe her horse, to grab at the threads of her shattered composure. 'I can't have anything else go wrong this year,' she said to him now.

She couldn't smile to soften her harsh words. Fire and ice alternately burned through her as she tried to blink away images of Lincoln's broken body lying on the ground beneath pounding hooves. 'Let's get back to work.'

She turned back to the yard and the work she wished would consume her. But no matter how frenetic, messy and physically demanding it proved to be, it didn't stop the sudden knowledge that had burst into her consciousness from pounding at her.

The fear that had gripped her when she'd thought Lincoln would be hurt...

The darkness that had engulfed her at the thought of him dying...

She'd gone and done the unthinkable. She'd fallen in love with her husband.

When they returned to the homestead that evening, Rose and Lincoln both went in separate directions.

Rose headed straight for her room to shower, pulled on her baggiest, most comfortable track pants and a fleece jumper, and collapsed to the side of her bed to try and make sense of the day's events. She'd fallen in love with Lincoln Garrison—the bad boy next door.

Only, he wasn't bad. He was... She rubbed her hands over her face. He was wonderful. Other than that daft risking-his-neck thing.

What are you going to do about it?

She had no idea.

She waited for one of the many voices she carried inside her to offer an opinion or advice—Pop, Grandma, Mum... Dad—but they all remained infuriatingly silent. She could talk to Eve...

She dismissed that thought as soon as she'd had

it. Her sister should be focussed on the arrival of her new baby, on married bliss with Nate. Evie deserved all her current happiness. Rose wasn't casting a shadow on it.

Besides, she had a feeling that this was something she needed to work out for herself.

On impulse, she made her way through the house, across the pristine white carpet of the piano bar, to open the door to the master suite. Her parents' marriage hadn't been perfect, but their love had survived all that life, and their own mistakes, had thrown at them. Could she and Lincoln do that too?

'I've never felt for any woman what I feel for you.'

He'd practically told her he was ready to settle down. Maybe...

She dragged both hands back through her hair. Once they'd had a chance to cool off and a decent night's sleep...and she apologised for shouting at him in front of everyone, and he promised never to be so reckless again... Well, maybe the two of them could make a go of their marriage as her parents had.

She turned on the spot. It was time to look to the future. It was time for her to take her rightful place here at Garrison Downs. No matter how much she missed her father, she was now station manager. It was time she embraced the role fully.

* * *

Rose woke to someone knocking on the French doors of her bedroom. 'Rose, wake up.'

Aaron.

She was up in an instant. Grabbing her robe, she flew across the room to fling the door open. 'What's happened?'

He grimaced.

'Come on, Aaron, out with it.' Had the stock in the yards broken free? Been stolen? Did someone need medical attention?

'Something fishy is going on.'

She breathed a little easier. Not an immediate emergency then, but something that worried him enough to wake her in the middle of the night. A glance at the clock told her it was only eleven p.m.— not that late, then. A glance at the bed confirmed what she already knew. For the first time in a month, she'd slept alone. She forced her gaze back to Aaron. 'Go on.'

'You're not going to like it, but I've been keeping my eye on Linc.'

She resisted the urge to roll her eyes. Of course he had.

'He just took off in his car. Headlights turned off.'

He'd left? Without telling her? Her throat tightened into a painful ache. He'd thrown in the towel because she'd yelled at him?

You didn't just yell at him. You called him awful names and were totally unreasonable.

'And headed west.'

Her head came up. Kalku Hills was south-east.

'I'm going to follow. Thought you might like to come along.'

Oh, she was coming along all right, if for no other reason than to prevent this pair from coming to blows. 'I'll get dressed.'

They drove for forty minutes before they saw Lincoln's car parked by the fence that ran parallel to the road to Marni. On the other side of the fence was a car with a horse float. Aaron flashed their car's headlights to high beam, and Lincoln and his father were caught in its glare. Lincoln's hand rested on the gate of the horse float. A pair of wire cutters hung from his other hand.

They hadn't spoken on their return to the homestead. She should've searched him out and cleared the air. But she'd still been trying to wrap her head around the fact that she'd fallen in love with him. And the thought of him walking away when she told him… She hadn't been able to face it.

The mental toing and froing coupled with the labour of the day had left her exhausted. She'd thought it might do them both good to gain some perspective first. Instead, had Lincoln been concocting some elaborate form of revenge?

Her chest cramped. Had he rung Clay and told him he'd had enough, and it was time to move on whatever their plan happened to be—to steal her cattle? The thought left her feeling broken.

Show no weakness.

All of the voices she held in her heart united to impart that single piece of advice.

Show no weakness.

Hauling in a breath, she straightened. Very slowly, she pushed out of the car. 'Evening, gentlemen.' She ambled over, but everything inside her trembled. The fence remained between them. 'Would someone like to tell me what's going on?'

Lincoln stared at her, his eyes burning. 'Rose, this isn't what it looks like.'

Beside her, Aaron folded his arms. 'What does it look like?'

Nobody spoke. Her heart thudded so hard she thought they must hear it.

Clay snarled. 'No one can accuse me of anything.'

Aaron jumped the fence, pushing past both men to stare into the back of the horse trailer. 'Two steers.' He came back to stand beside Rose. 'Diseased, by the look of it.'

Clay had been planning to place diseased cattle on her property? But… Why on earth would he risk that disease then spreading to his own herd? Because it would. Eventually.

Leaning against a fencepost as if she hadn't a care in the world, she surveyed the older man. Fatigue threatened to swallow her whole. The act was senseless. He might hate the Waverlys, but he wouldn't do something so against his own interests. He shifted and she noted the cold calculation in his eyes. The…triumph?

She stilled. His hatred hadn't become mindless. Not yet. Her mind raced. He'd already achieved what he wanted to achieve.

Which was…*what*, exactly?

Clay clapped his son on the shoulder. 'C'mon, Linc, time to go home. I told you this would all end in tears. We'll get you a quickie divorce. And then we'll let the courts decide what to do about Holt's will.'

And then she saw it—Clay's plan. Lincoln had been set up. She and Aaron had been meant to find Lincoln and Clay like this.

For a moment she trembled. If she was wrong…

CHAPTER THIRTEEN

A BONE-DEEP WEARINESS descended over Lincoln, and he had to fight an urge to brace his hands on his knees. He'd ruined *everything*.

Rose had told him how fragile their trust was. He'd sworn he wouldn't break it. But he'd come out here on his own when Jackson had told him that something was going down. He should've brought her with him. He should've told her what he was doing.

She'd never believe him. Not now.

And he couldn't blame her. He knew exactly what it looked like. Diseased cattle. Wire cutters in his hand.

An invisible vice squeezed his ribs tight until he couldn't breathe, until he thought they might crack.

Hell, talk about *pathetic*. He hadn't brought her with him because he'd still been smarting from the dressing-down she'd given him this afternoon. And she'd been right to. Dashing amid flying hooves to save her bracelet had been foolhardy. But he knew what that bracelet meant to her. And he'd do it again in a heartbeat. He'd been playing the hero for her.

Again.

She'd told him she didn't need a hero, but that was exactly what he wanted to be—her hero. But in coming out alone tonight he'd acted like one of those stupid, insecure men on the soaps she so loved.

She didn't need one of those.

She didn't need a hero either. What she needed was an equal partner who'd be honest with her.

And he'd blown it.

He'd played directly into his father's hands, and he couldn't blame her for having no faith in him now. He'd come out here to prevent his father from doing something he'd regret, help him save face without anyone else present. But Clay didn't deserve that kind of consideration. Another serious lack of judgement on Lincoln's part.

A grey and featureless future stretched out in front of him. The chance of winning Rose's heart might now be lost to him, but his father had another thing coming if he thought Linc was just going to fall in with his plans. Rose might no longer want him, but he wasn't divorcing her, not before she was ready.

Too soon or not, he wished with every atom that he'd told her he loved her.

He opened his mouth, but Rose spoke first. 'I'm afraid that will cost your son dearly, Clay. You see, he signed a contract giving me the Cessna, Thunder and Colin if he didn't keep his side of our bargain. And just so we're clear, his side of the bargain is to remain married to me.'

She leaned her elbows on the fence post and oh-so-casually rested her chin in her hand. She'd never looked more beautiful.

'And you know what? I'm not sure that's a price he's willing to pay.'

Clay's face twisted as he swung to Linc. 'You stupid idiot! What the hell were you—?'

Clay raised a hand. In a flash, Rose was over the fence and between them, her hand in the centre of Clay's chest pushing him back. 'Lay one finger on my husband, Clay, and I will deck you.'

Clay blinked. So did Linc.

'If you don't think Holt taught me how to fight then you'd be the idiot. And while you are a truly reprehensible human being, I don't think even you would hit a woman.'

Clay lowered his arm. 'Of course I wouldn't hit a woman.'

'Which means you'd just have to stand there and take it while I whipped your butt.'

He glanced at Linc. 'You going to let her speak to me like that?'

Linc shrugged and tried to keep the grin from his face. He didn't need a hero either, but he sure as hell liked watching Rose play one. 'I reckon you deserve it.'

'Why do you continue being such a pig-headed idiot? Why aren't you boasting about Lincoln's accomplishments near and far rather than putting him down all the time? Why won't you acknowledge his true worth?'

Her hands clenched into fists and Lincoln readied to grab her around the waist in case she did take a swing at Clay.

Those fists unclenched and she turned to Aaron. 'Did you know Lincoln topped his year at university, has a doctorate and has co-authored a textbook on economic theory?'

Aaron's jaw dropped.

'He advises government officials on how to best invest the nation's capital to benefit the economy, and yet his father ignores his advice, freely given, something that I'd happily pay for.'

Clay glared at them all. 'You know nothing!'

'What I know is that you love playing the poor put-upon victim—*"Oh, my wife left me!" "Oh, my son is off partying and neglecting his duties at home." "Oh, if only Cordelia hadn't gambled away Garrison Downs."*'

Clay took a step towards her, but Lincoln and Aaron stepped together to provide a defensive wall. Clay's face twisted and he stabbed a finger at them. 'Garrison Downs should be mine.'

'There was no poker match, Dad.'

He'd spent too much of his life feeling bad for his father, pitying him, trying to make up life's disappointments to him. It hadn't done an ounce of good. Clay refused to acknowledge what was good in his life, preferring to focus on his sense of injury. 'Cordelia *didn't* gamble it away.'

Clay took an unsteady step back. 'You found the diary?'

'Letters, not a diary. Letters Cordelia and Louisa May wrote to each other. They were friends, not enemies. And the land was Cordelia's in her own right. It didn't belong to her brother, Arthur—it never had. He'd already gambled his grandfather's inheritance away.'

'Lies,' Clay croaked.

'Cordelia gave the land to Lissy May for saving her life three times and to cover a debt of her brother's. She spread the rumour of the poker match to get rid of an unwanted suitor. There was no cheating, no lying. The two women were the best of friends.'

Rose pushed between him and Aaron to stand beside them. 'The reason Kalku Hills isn't as big a success as Garrison Downs is because *you* don't know how to put in a proper day's work. It's easier to whine than it is to work.'

Clay's jaw dropped.

'You don't make the best use of Kalku Hills' resources.'

'Now, look here—'

'And your biggest mistake was in not listening to Lincoln's ideas for improvements, because you couldn't bear to think he might know better than you. You can bet your bottom dollar I won't be making that same mistake.'

Linc stilled.

'I might lack my father's freakish business brain. Genius like that rarely comes along. But I mean to play to my strengths and I know what they are. For one, I'm an excellent judge of character.'

Her hand slid about Linc's upper arm and she held on as though she never meant to let go. His heart thundered like a galloping horse.

'And I know my land—every inch of it.'

'I—'

'And I might lack my father's wheeling-and-dealing charisma and know-how, but Lincoln doesn't.'

Clay stiffened, and in those few words Linc realised Rose had brought home to his father all that his folly and bitterness had cost him.

'Now this is what's going to happen.'

She sounded every inch the boss and he bit back a grin.

She pointed to Clay. 'If you come onto my land again to scatter my cattle to the four winds, I will report you to the police.'

Before his father could respond she swung to Aaron. 'And if I find out you've gone onto Kalku Hills land to do the same, I will fire you.'

Aaron's head rocked back. 'Whoa, steady on, I—'

'I mean it!'

She glared at both men. God, she was magnificent. How could she have ever doubted her ability to step into Holt's shoes?

'I don't care what the provocation, this stupid feud ends with this generation. Do you hear me?'

Aaron shuffled his feet and finally nodded. 'Aye, Boss.'

His words reflected the new-found respect in his eyes. Linc silently applauded her.

'And the other thing that's going to happen, Clay, is that you're taking those steers to the vet in Marni tonight and having them treated.'

'That'll cost me a packet—'

'You should've thought about that before you started this charade. Those animals don't deserve to suffer more than they already have.'

Aaron nodded. 'Agreed, and I think I might just go along with Clay to make sure that happens.'

'Before you head off…' Linc's gaze collided with his father's '… I want to know who your informant at Garrison Downs is.'

Rose tightened her grip on his arm. 'I've worked that out.'

She had?

Both their gazes moved to Aaron.

Aaron's eyes widened. 'It's not me!'

Rose nodded. 'I know.'

Linc stared. It wasn't? Then who…?

'Think about it, Aaron.'

She blew out a breath, looking suddenly tired, and he had to fight an urge to pull her into his arms.

He watched the other man turn options over in his mind.

'Who has had access to Holt's study to copy documents we wouldn't want shared?'

He saw the moment the realisation hit.

'Lindy,' Aaron croaked.

Damn.

'I'm sorry. I know the two of you have become close. I don't know why she'd jeopardise her position like that. It's a shame. I liked her.'

Aaron dragged a hand down his face. 'Money. Her mother is in a nursing home. It's costing her a fortune.' He pulled in a breath. 'Rose, look… she doesn't have a bad heart, I swear.'

Rose stared, eventually nodded. 'Decent people can do bad things when they're under a lot of stress.'

A lesson she'd learned from her own family.

'We'll see if we can sort something out.'

Aaron let out a breath. 'Thanks, Rose.' He turned back to Clay. 'Come on, let's go.'

Lincoln didn't watch them leave. He only had eyes for Rose.

Rose watched the tail lights of Clay's horse float disappear into the night. Only then did she turn to face Lincoln. How much of herself had she given away in her defence of him? And would he use it against her?

He's a better man than that.

'Rose, I—'

He halted when she held up a hand. 'I'm sorry I hauled you over the coals like I did out at the yards this afternoon. I shouldn't have said what I did. And I shouldn't have said it in front of everyone. I was no better than your father.'

'You're *nothing* like my father, Rose. In your shoes I'd have done exactly the same. And,' he added when she opened her mouth, 'you're forgiven.'

His eyes glittered in the starlight and she wanted him with a fierceness that took her off guard.

'I thought you were going to kick me to the kerb just then.' His chest heaved as if dragging in a much-needed breath. 'I thought you were going to send me packing.'

The ragged lines of his face and the slope of his shoulders told her that thought had gutted him. He *did* care for her. Her heart picked up speed. Given time, could she earn his love and make this temporary marriage permanent? 'Nuh uh. I bought you. I own you. That's a line from *Groundhog Day*, by the way. And I know I don't really—'

The rest of her words were cut off when large hands cupped her face and tilted it up to meet the demands of firm, lean lips. It was a kiss that turned her world upside down.

She swayed.

She moaned.

She opened her mouth and let him have all of her.

'I don't care if it's too soon or not.' He lifted his head, his breathing ragged, his voice raspy. 'I don't mean to spook you or freak you out, but I love you, Rose. I've always loved you.'

He… Wait, *what*?

'I've spent my whole life watching you, admiring you. And, as soon as puberty hit, lusting after you.'

Her jaw dropped, but her heart lifted, took flight like a majestic wedge-tailed eagle. 'No way,' she breathed.

'Yes way.'

He released her, leaving her strangely untethered.

'But things between our families were…'

'Complicated.' She nodded.

'And I was a couple of years older than you and I…'

'You what?' He'd only ever asked her out on one date. He'd never told her he was crazy about her.

That he loved her.

'I wanted to wait until you'd finished university and had seen a bit of the world—experienced a bit of the world.'

He bent down until they were eye to eye. She ached to touch him.

'I never expected to be your first lover, Rose, but I sure as hell wanted to be your last one.'

Her pulse…her heart…everything raced and danced and swooned. It took a force of will to drag air into lungs that didn't want to work; to make sense of all he was saying.

'If you felt that way, why didn't you ask me out on another date?' The words burst from her like an accusation.

'A date you turned down, let me remind you.'

More fool her. But…would she have been ready for all of this seven years ago?

'And you asked me—begged me—to never ask you again.'

Oh, God, she had.

'I hate men like Cordelia's Geoffrey Bannister. I never wanted to become someone like that. I had no intention of badgering you. You'd said no, and I had to respect that.'

She couldn't move, couldn't speak…could only stare.

'But I knew it was inevitable that we'd see each other throughout the year. And every single time I'd make a point of seeking you out, to say hello, to flirt a little.'

'I remember.'

'You never gave me any encouragement, but I refused to give up hope that one day you might.'

She'd been too afraid to, had never in a million years thought he could be serious about her.

'But when you asked me to marry you, I finally had an opportunity to prove we belonged together. You'd given me three months and I meant to make the most of them and win your heart.'

Her eyes burned. She pressed her hand to his cheek. How had she ever managed to deserve this wonderful man?

'I nearly destroyed it all when you told me you were a virgin.'

She grimaced. 'I thought my revelation had turned you off.'

'I was so angry with your grandmother for extracting such a promise. But more than that I was appalled at my own reaction—a kind of primitive possessiveness.'

He raked a hand through his hair and paced in front of her. 'I wanted to leave some kind of mark on you that declared you mine. As if I was some alpha wolf or something. I wanted you so badly I was afraid I'd hurt you. And I wanted our first time to be special. Something you could always look back on with fondness.'

Shaking his head, he halted in front of her. 'I needed to get my head back on straight. I didn't stop to think what message I might be sending you. I was such an idiot.'

'*Not* an idiot.' She gave a low laugh. 'I feel as if our relationship has been one step forward and three steps back, but it's been worth it. All we've been through has forced me to acknowledge the kind of man you are. And I like that man.'

His eyes blazed in his face. 'Are you saying I have a chance at winning your heart?'

He hadn't realised…?

She raised both hands heavenward. 'Why do you think I lost my temper so completely this afternoon? I was so afraid of you being hurt…or worse. I knew I was beginning to care, but that… *That* was the moment I realised I was in love with you. And it scared me witless.'

He stared as if her words made no sense and then his hands curved around her shoulders and he was lifting her onto her tiptoes. 'Say that again.'

'I love you, Lincoln. You're the best man I've ever known. You do your best to look after everyone—and you do it in kind, subtle, and unconfrontational ways. You don't ask for fanfare or acknowledgement. You just see what needs doing and you do it. You're honest and honourable, and you know what those things mean to me. If I was given the tools and the power, I couldn't create a man who would suit me better. You're perfect for me. And I want to be perfect for you.'

He stared at her as if he couldn't get enough of her and the words she was whispering to him. This beautiful man had never had anyone truly appreciate him. But she would if he let her. A tear spilled from her eye and then another. She'd appreciate and love him until her dying day.

He thumbed away her tears. 'Don't cry, Rose.'

The words were a whisper on the night air. 'Happy tears,' she whispered back. He deserved so much more than he'd ever been given. He deserved everything. 'When I get too serious, Lincoln, you make me laugh. When I get too caught up in work, you distract me and make me see all the wonders around me. You make my life so much better. And this may be shallow, but I love what you look like, I love your body. And making love with you is my very favourite thing.'

She found herself suddenly released.

She swayed. He was supposed to kiss her now, not release her!

In the red dirt in front of her, he went down on one knee. She pressed trembling fingers to her mouth. Reaching up, he took her hands in his. 'Back at the homestead, hidden in the depths of a drawer, is the engagement ring I bought for you and swore I'd give to you before our temporary three-month marriage was up. I had it especially designed so you could wear it while you work—flat so it won't catch on anything—a yellow diamond set in platinum. I see it and I think of you—strong, enduring and beautiful.' His grip on her hands tightened. 'Rose, will you do me the very great honour of agreeing to being my *forever* wife?'

'Yes!'

The word rang out in the silence of the night and his grin was *everything*. Bending down, she kissed him, and then she was in his arms and he was whooping and spinning her around and she'd never known it was possible to be so happy.

Later, much later, stretched out beside him in her bed, she lifted her hand to admire the way the diamond caught the moonlight. 'It's the most beautiful ring I've ever seen.'

Catching her hand, Lincoln kissed it, before folding it against his chest. 'If I'd known Ana designed jewellery, I'd have commissioned her to make it.'

'Except she'd have told me and let the cat out of the bag.' Propping her head on her hand, she stared down at him. 'How would you feel if I commissioned her to make us new wedding rings? These ones were just a prop.' She gestured to the ones that they wore.

'Prop or not, this one means a lot to me.' He twisted it around on his finger. 'Could she melt some of this gold into the new rings?'

'Of course she can. She's a marvel.' She stared at her wedding ring then too. 'That's a nice idea.' A symbol of how their relationship had evolved.

He reached up and kissed her. 'Now tell me what else is going through that beautiful head of yours?'

He read her so well. 'How would you feel if we had a ceremony renewing our vows? I want everyone to know that I love you. I want them to know you're my family—that I've chosen you because there's not a better man alive for me, that I want you as the father of my children, and that I want you at my side for the rest of my life.'

Reaching up, he kissed her again—slowly and oh-so-thoroughly—and then she was on her back and he was moving above her and they were moving as one and it was a long time before either of them spoke again.

'That was a yes, by the way,' he said when their breathing had returned to normal. 'I love you, Rose. Forever.'

She met his gaze and smiled with all of herself. 'Forever.'

EPILOGUE

Garrison Downs,
mid-September

ROSE STARED AT her three sisters—all here together *in person* at Garrison Downs for the first time in what felt like forever—and her heart expanded until it felt too big for her chest.

Evie, Tilly and Ana sat side by side on the swing chattering like bright and bubbly rainbow lorikeets in their wedding blessing finery. A lump lodged in Rose's throat. Tilly, glancing up, caught her expression and nudged the others. They all quietened like schoolgirls in a classroom and it made her smile because their demure exteriors didn't fool her for a moment.

'Right, I'm now calling this meeting to order.' She pressed her hands together. 'I love you guys.' Despite her best efforts, her eyes filled. 'I know you know that, but I love you bigger than my own heart.'

'Oh, God, Rose, stop!' Evie pressed hands to her cheeks. 'You'll have me ruining my make-up.'

'Make-up, schmake-up,' Tilly scorned. 'It's our party and we can cry if we want to.'

Ana held up a small make-up bag. 'We can touch up.' Her grin grew shy. 'I brought it along just in case.'

Tilly wrapped Ana in a hug. Evie winked at Rose. 'Guess you have free rein, then, Boss.'

Rose met her sisters' gazes one by one. 'I love each of you more than I love Garrison Downs. I know you're all aware what this station means to me—Garrison Downs is my life. But each of you, as well as Lincoln and the families we're all creating, are my heart.'

Their eyes welled then too and Rose's vision blurred, and though she blinked hard, it refused to clear. 'I never expected any of you to marry so that we could keep the station.' She gave a shaky laugh. 'So that *I* could keep the station. Only now that we have, I can't tell you how happy I am that we did, because the men we've married are not only hard-working, honourable and decent—'

'Don't forget hot,' Evie piped in.

'*So* hot,' Tilly crooned.

'Dreamy,' Ana murmured.

Lincoln's powerful form rose in her mind and she found herself grinning. 'I could *never* forget that, but… They love us in the way we deserve to be loved—with all of themselves. And I couldn't want more for us in life partners. Not in a million years could I have imagined such a happy outcome.' She pressed her hands to her heart. 'Thank you. From the bottom of my heart, thank you.'

And then her sisters swooped on her as one, and they were group-hugging and crying and murmuring loving nonsense, and it made Rose's heart sing.

When they'd dried their eyes and had retouched each other's make-up, Rose said, 'Don't forget that Garrison Downs is your home. You're building other homes too—homes where you're loved and where you belong, and that's as it should be. But don't forget the Downs will always be here for you. And I'm very much hoping we can manage at least one in four Christmases here.'

Linking pinkies, they made a pact.

'I have one final announcement to make.' She pulled in a deep breath. Her three sisters promptly sat on the swing again. 'Lincoln has had his father sign a statutory declaration relinquishing any claim the Garrison family have to this land.'

Tilly clapped her hands. 'He is such a good guy!'

'How?' Evie gaped. 'Clay is a—'

'I know!' Rose cut in before Evie could call him something horrible. The man *was* her father-in-law. 'Lincoln told him that if he wanted to mend their relationship, that's what he had to do.' To her utter amazement, Clay had acquiesced without a murmur.

Ana's eyes shone. 'Good for him!'

'If you're all in agreement, I'll have the will changed so that no future generation of Waverly women find themselves in the same predicament we did. We've been ridiculously fortunate, and I wouldn't change a thing about these past fifteen months, but I don't want my daughters or their daughters facing that same dilemma we did. All in agreement of having that conditional bequest removed, please raise your hand.'

Four hands shot in the air.

Perfect.

'Okay, is there any other order of business?'

'Me! Me!' Tilly leapt up.

Rose took her vacated spot on the swing, linking arms with Evie and Ana.

'Louisa May's and Cordelia's letters have been officially verified. They're definitely legitimate, dating back to the early nineteen hundreds—and all is true and correct. Louisa May and Cordelia were besties, sisters of the heart, and I think we should sing that out loud and proud to the rest of the world.'

They all cheered.

'Anyone else have anything to say?' Tilly moved to lean against the swing, a hand circling its chain.

'I don't need to stand to say it,' Evie said. 'I just want you all to know I'm so glad to be home. I never knew I could find so much *happiness* here.'

Rose squeezed her sister's arm. 'You're back where you belong, Bambi.'

'I get jealous sometimes when I think of the two of you here.' Tilly let out a gusty sigh. 'And then I remember I'm a princess living in a castle with my prince charming...' She trailed off, making them all laugh.

Ana shot to her feet. 'I want to say something.'

Tilly promptly took her seat, her arm twining through Rose's.

'I just... I want to say... Well, just that I'm so glad you found out about me, so glad you're my sisters.'

'And we are too!'

And then there was more hugging, followed perhaps by a little more necessary touching-up of their make-up.

'So,' Rose finally said, 'are we ready to do this?'

'Yes,' her sisters chorused.

Arm in arm they walked around to Rosamund's glorious rose garden. One by one they walked down the aisle towards their respective husbands—Prince Henri, Nathan, Connor, and Lincoln—who watched them with steady, intent eyes. The late afternoon air was filled with the sounds of birdcalls, the scent of spring and the happy sighs of all who were present.

In front of the people who mattered to them most—family and friends, and the entire township of Marni—they renewed their wedding vows, their voices clear, strong and sure. After the wedding blessing a cheer went up from the assembled crowd. Photos were taken and congratulations flowed and then people began to move in the direction of the ballroom for the celebration banquet.

Before they could follow, Granny Lavigne came up with the latest addition to the family, Evie and Nate's daughter, Hope—the most adorable bundle of blonde hair, chubby legs, and the trademark Waverly blue eyes. Granny Lavigne kissed them all and told them how proud and happy she was for them.

Rose glanced at the nearby roses.

We miss you, she silently told her parents. *We love you.*

Tilly gave an excited wriggle. 'I can't wait until my little bundle of joy meets you all.' She and Henri had announced that they were expecting a baby in March. There'd been much celebration at the news.

'Ana?' Tilly nudged their youngest sister.

'Clucky,' she admitted. 'Working on it.'

Ana's family—her mum, Lili, and her grandparents—immediately started talking at once. Rose grinned. They were quickly becoming some of her favourite people. She was beyond glad that they'd come to Garrison Downs…that old hurts were being healed.

'Rose?'

Evie's voice hauled her back and she found all eyes had turned to her. She touched a gentle finger to her new niece's cheek. 'Well, as I don't like long being outdone by you lot…' Across their heads she met Lincoln's gaze. His grin made her heart swell. 'I guess I'll probably start working on it too.'

'Our babies will be the best of friends.' That was Tilly.

Evie's eyes danced. 'They'll be trouble. Into all the mischief.'

'But in the best way.' Ana grinned.

'And we'll love every moment,' Rose agreed. 'But they're not allowed in the piano bar until they're at least sixteen.'

Laughing, they made their way towards the ballroom to dance and celebrate the night away.

Later, as Rose danced a sedate number with Aaron, they passed the table where Lincoln's father Clay held court and overheard him brag that it'd be his grandchildren who would one day run Garrison Downs. 'Surprised he has the gall to show his face,' Aaron said with a growl.

'Lincoln told him he'd not be welcome today until he apologised to me. Which he did—comprehensively, too. I think he was genuinely ashamed of himself.' A truce had been called and she was grateful for it. 'I think Dad's death sent him off the rails for a bit.'

Aaron grimaced. 'Holt's death sent us all into a spin. I know I've apologised—'

'No more apologies!'

He cleared his throat, nodded. 'I don't know how to say this without sounding patronising, but... I'm proud of you, Rose. You've single-handedly dragged everything back from the brink and we're now as productive as we've ever been. You've filled shoes I never thought could be filled.'

'I didn't do it single-handedly. I've had all of you working with me, just like Holt did.'

Aaron held her gaze. 'Holt's very best legacy is his daughters. He'd be so proud of you.'

She blinked hard, swallowed. 'Thanks, Aaron. Now, I think it's time for you to go and find Lindy. I told her she wasn't to work tonight, but she keeps ducking into the kitchens.'

'She wants the night to be perfect. She's just doing what she can to make amends. She's so grateful you've let her stay. I am too.'

That one act had won her Aaron's and Lindy's undying loyalty and she didn't regret it for a moment. She pushed him in the direction of the kitchen. 'Go dance with your girl.'

When she turned, she found Lincoln standing behind her. Without a word he pulled her into his arms and they swayed together in perfect harmony. Had she ever known a moment of such perfect contentment?

'I have something I want to show you.' Lincoln led her through to the primary suite, which they'd finally made their own.

She waggled her eyebrows. 'Oh?'

A low chuckle left his throat. 'Behave, woman. I have a wedding present for you.'

She pulled him to a halt. 'You already gave me a wedding present.'

'This is another one.'

She loved her chess set—her *well-used* chess set. 'Can I say something first?'

He immediately stopped trying to shift her forward. 'Always.'

From where they stood, she could see a corner of the bed and its quilt of muted greens, pinks and golds. In the daytime those colours were reflected in the view from the picture window—lush green lawns, towering gums with olive leaves and pink blossoms, and, further beyond, the golden grasses and red dirt.

Home. Their home.

'I'm grateful every single day that you said yes when I asked you to marry me.'

His face gentled. He opened his mouth but she touched fingers to his lips. 'Marrying you is the single best thing I've ever done. The best,' she added firmly, when he frowned. 'Knowing you, loving you, being loved by you, has filled all of the spaces inside me that I never knew were empty. Thank you, Lincoln. Thank you for being patient with me, for not giving up on me, and for loving me.' Reaching up on tiptoe, she kissed him, and he kissed her back with an intensity that had her clinging to him.

Pulling back, his breathing ragged, he shook his head. 'You have the ability to undo me every single time.'

'Not true.' Her breathing was just as ragged. 'You're currently ahead in our chess tournament.' Because of course they were keeping count.

'Only by the skin of my teeth.'

As he spoke he ushered her forward, gestured at a simple frame hanging on the wall. She moved across to read it. 'This is the contract you had drawn up giving me Judy, Thunder and Colin. I gave it back to you. We—'

'It's a symbol of the fact that I'm all in, Rose.'

She turned back to him. 'I know you are.'

'You're sharing so much with me—your home, for a start.'

She cocked her head to one side. 'Well, my portion of it at least.' She placed her hand over his heart. 'We're family now. We share everything.'

He gestured at the frame before gathering her close. 'I never want you to forget that it's *you* that is most important in my life. I love the home we're creating, I already love the children we're going to make, and I love being a part of your already existing family, but it's *you*, Rose. None of it means anything without you.'

Some days she had to pinch herself to believe this amazing man was hers. 'I feel the same way.'

A lazy grin stretched across his face. 'I also thought, in a similar vein to Louisa May's and Cordelia's letters, it could go in the family archive to amuse the generations to come.'

She started to laugh, imagining the tall tales they'd spin for their children.

Glancing at the bed and then at him, she raised an eyebrow that had him chuckling. 'Later. You can't leave the party early when you're the belle of the ball. And make no mistake, Rose, you are queen of Garrison Downs.'

'And you're my king.'

His eyes danced and he gave one of those slow lazy smiles. 'Prince consort will do fine for me, as long as I'm king of your heart.'

'Always,' she promised. Before pointing to the contract on the wall. 'You're mine.'

'You bought me,' he agreed, dark eyes filled with laughter.

'And then you won my heart.'

He sobered. 'I'm never giving it back.'

'And I'm never letting you go.'

'Checkmate,' they said at the same time.

His head lowered to hers. 'Forever,' he whispered against her lips.

'And ever and ever,' she agreed, before his lips claimed hers in another toe-tingling kiss.

* * * * *

*If you missed the previous story in
the One Year to Wed quartet
then check out*

Cinderella and the Tycoon Next Door
by Kandy Shepherd

*And if you enjoyed this story, check out these
other great reads from Michelle Douglas*

Waking Up Married to the Billionaire
Cinderella's Secret Fling
Unbuttoning the Tuscan Tycoon

All available now!

HARLEQUIN
Reader Service

Enjoyed your book?

Try the perfect subscription for Romance readers and get more great books like this delivered right to your door.

See why over 10+ million readers have tried Harlequin Reader Service.

Start with a Free Welcome Collection with free books and a gift—valued over $20.

Choose any series in print or ebook.
See website for details and order today:

TryReaderService.com/subscriptions